Pack of Lies

Roz Levens

For Kathy -
Hope you enjoy it!

ROZevens x

Pack of Lies
Roz Levens

Edited by Black Pear Press

First published in June 2020 by Black Pear Press
www.blackpear.net

Copyright © Roz Levens

All rights reserved.

ISBN 978-1-913418-13-7

Cover Photograph by Tim Price at Pricewrite.co.uk

Black Pear Press

For Tim, who knows when to interrupt with a cup of tea and when to back away silently...

Part One

The Letter

The envelope was stiff, like junk mail, but addressed by hand. Unremarkable, it could have gone straight into the recycling. It lurked at the bottom of Tuesday's mail, with all the other tedious, everyday stuff: a flyer from a pizza joint; a "golden opportunity" to invest in a new, gated retirement village; a reminder from the dentist; she nearly didn't bother opening it. Later, she wondered what would have happened if she'd just chucked it into the shredder. She'd opened it.

Inside was an old, slightly creased, black and white photograph, obviously taken at a wedding. The bride, in a plunging, sequinned skin tight little number, was laughing up at the grinning groom, who bore a striking resemblance to a younger version of Sara's own husband, Graham. Something made her look harder, and then with her heart pounding, she turned the photograph over. Printed neatly on the back were six words that turned her world upside down.

"Micaela and Graham, 14 February 1997."

1997. Sara froze. Her mind refused to compute. It couldn't possibly be Graham. She stared at the familiar face again, her brain whirling. In February 1997, she and Graham had already been married for five years. At that time, she had been going through her second round of IVF and he had been working all the hours

God sent to try and pay for it. Working away from home, for weeks at a time, on one key deal after another.

Her hands shaking slightly, Sara forced herself to look at the image again. The bride in the picture was very young. She was pretty, too, in an overblown way. Her neckline was too low, her slick black eyeliner too heavy, and her painted nails far too long. Her shiny dark hair had been piled up into a mass of curls and crowned with a glitzy tiara. Giant chandeliers of crystal hung from each earlobe, flashing in the winter sun. In short, she was the epitome of everything that Graham always maintained he hated most in a woman. The picture was only in black and white, but Sara could tell by the contrast her skin made with the wedding dress, that the bride must have had a heavy spray tan.

Sara caught a glimpse of herself in the long hall mirror. Her reflection revealed a shortish, middle-aged woman with neat blonde hair, minimal make up and pale skin. The only jewellery she wore was a thick gold band on the third finger of her left hand, and simple gold studs in the shape of plaited knots in her earlobes. Her navy trousers and cream shirt were expensive, well cut, immaculately pressed, and suitable for any situation: a wedding; a funeral; work; shopping; lunch with friends, and her navy leather court shoes were smart, tending towards the sensible. "Professional" might be the first word people conjured up when meeting her. Or understated, perhaps. Invisible in a crowd, certainly. A less kind person might even use the word dull.

The woman in the photograph would never be invisible. Heads would turn wherever she went, blousy or not. What the hell was Graham doing with her?

Sara's confusion began to recede, and an icy white burn of utter fury started in her gut, rising like a volcano inside her. She tipped her head back and roared, no words, just brute anguish. Arthur, the neighbourhood cat leapt off her windowsill where he'd been snoozing, making the cat flap rattle crazily in his escape, his exit crossing with the pounding feet of Wendy from next door. As usual, she let herself in without knocking, bursting into the kitchen and staring up the hall at Sara.

'Jesus, Sara. What on earth's happened? Are you OK? You scared me half to death.'

Wordlessly, her heart pounding, Sara walked quickly into the kitchen, her heels clicking on the pale woodblock floor. She thrust the photograph at Wendy. 'Tell me, do you recognise the groom?' Her voice didn't waver.

'No. Oh, wait, though—hang on, he looks like your Graham, a bit, doesn't he?'

'You might think that. Try reading the back of the picture.'

Wendy flipped the picture over, and then looked up, puzzled. Sara watched the penny drop.

'No, look, this is wrong, surely? Someone's winding you up—this is a joke, isn't it?'

'I'd say it was a joke, yes.' She heard scathing sarcasm in her own voice.

'I meant…'

'I know what you meant.' Sara knew her face was tense with anger, her eyes flashing with barely controlled fury. 'However, Graham Edward Parker promised to love and to cherish ME, forsaking all others, on October 17, 1992. Which means, if my memory serves me correctly, that when that picture was taken in February 1997, on Valentine's Day, no less,' here her voice dripped with bitterness, 'I was in the John Radcliffe Hospital in Oxford, going through yet another unsuccessful round of IVF.'

'Oh, Sara.' Ever maternal, Wendy started towards her friend, her arms reaching out.

'No.' She turned away. 'No, for God's sake, don't be nice to me. Sympathy is the last thing I need right now. I have to look at this methodically; I need to use my brain, not my heart. I need to THINK…'

Wendy's arms dropped down to her sides helplessly. Automatically, she straightened the front of her snug silvery-green Minuet top, tucked her hair behind her ears and filled the kettle instead, finding mugs and teabags with long-practised familiarity. Sara was grateful for the space. She sat down by the window, staring into the middle distance, focusing on nothing, her brain whirling through the possibilities rapidly, and dismissing them just as quickly. Wendy put the two heavy pottery mugs on the table and pulling out the other Windsor chair, sat down opposite her, fiddling with the silver Tiffany necklace she was wearing, pulling the shiny little heart forward and back. The clicking noise that the pendant made as it slid over the chain links started to wind Sara up even more. She made a conscious effort

4

to unclench her teeth and relax her jaw—the effort ruined when Wendy spoke up again.

'When did you get the photo? Was it just pushed under your door, like in the movies?'

Sara held back the comment that was on the tip of her tongue. Wendy had been a good neighbour for years, but she did have a tendency to say the first vacuous thing that popped into her head. It was part of her appeal really, a welcome relief from all those careful, professional conversations that Sara had with clients and colleagues at work.

'It was in this morning's post with everything else. I thought it was just junk mail at first.'

'Bin it.' Wendy was practical, blunt as ever. 'It's someone playing a nasty trick. Our Tyler's really good with Photoshop, I bet if we showed it to him he'd be able to tell you how it'd been done. It's just a mean prank. Bin it, I would.' Tyler was Wendy's 15 year-old son. He never looked up, he never stood up straight if he could slump against something, and as far as Sara knew, he didn't speak. She'd heard him grunt, when prompted by Wendy—'Say hello to Sara, Tyler,'—but his responses had been similar to the sort you'd get if you prodded a pig with a stick. Wendy had once told Sara that she'd considered getting herself a frame made, like a giant iPhone, so that Tyler would at least look at her when she spoke to him.

'But why would anyone go to all the bother of doing something like this? It must be someone who knows me, why would anyone do that?'

'There's some funny buggers about. It might be

someone who knows Graham, stirring up a bit of trouble.' She peered more closely at the picture. 'It might even be her, this wedding girl, Miranda, was it?'

'Micaela.' The name sounded bitter on her tongue.

'Micaela. Odd name. Well, I've heard the name, of course, but I didn't think it was spelled like that. Foreign, is she?'

Sara's eyes narrowed, and biting back a second sharp reply, she shrugged, staying silent. She held the mug, from habit, but ignored the rapidly cooling tea, fixing her gaze on the top of the gently swirling liquid, seeing nothing.

'The thing is, Sara, d'you think it's for real? *Could* it be real? Did you ever get the idea that he might have someone else? Another woman?'

'No. Never. He's been a bit distracted from time-to-time, sure, but I've always put that down to pressure of work. And I guess we don't speak as often as we used to, but that's texting for you, isn't it? We all chat less than we used to, don't we?'

'I guess so.' Wendy paused, trying desperately to think of something helpful to say. 'Perhaps whatever this was is all over. This was years ago after all, and you're still together, aren't you?' She flapped the photo in the air. 'And maybe it wasn't real—perhaps it was taken for a play, or an advert, or something?'

Sara raised her eyebrows.

'Sorry. I know. Wittering. I was only trying to help.'

'I know.'

The women sipped their tea in silent contemplation. Sara cringed at the bitterness of the dark brown brew

6

that her friend always seemed to produce, no matter the quality of the tea. Wendy tried again.

'Do you have any idea where the picture was taken?'

'I suspect it was taken at a wedding, Wendy.'

The sarcasm was unmistakable. Wendy refused to rise to the jibe.

'I meant, can we see WHERE it is, on the picture?' She turned the photograph sideways on the table so they could both look at it.

Sara narrowed her eyes. In her heart of hearts she was shouting, 'Tart. Whore. Bitch,' but her lips were compressed into a tight closed line. Years of staying calm in meetings, where infuriating people constantly said stupid, thoughtless things, stood her in good stead. She breathed slowly, deeply, trying to get a grip on her jumbled thoughts. How had her day plummeted to such a degree that a picture of her beloved Graham, caring husband for 26 years, friend, confidant, lover, clown, had turned into cruel evidence? A single tear overspilled and slid down her cheek. She wiped it away angrily, hoping that Wendy hadn't spotted it.

'It's in England, I think.' Wendy was examining the picture minutely, oblivious to Sara's anguish. 'I can see part of a sign behind her, there, see?' She pointed out a few letters behind the bride's elbow.

'You're right, but what difference does it make?'

'Look at it this way, we know the date. We've got their names, well, his name anyway. If we can work out where this is, we could check it out. You can find out anything online. I Googled Theresa May's house yesterday.'

Sara resisted the distraction of asking, 'Why, for God's sake,' and considered the idea.

'The thing is, Wendy, he probably used a fake name. If this IS a real wedding photo, I mean. It's against the law to have two wives at the same time. It's called bi-gam-y.'

'I know you think I'm an idiot, Sara, but there's no need to treat me like one.'

'Sorry.' Sara closed her eyes and shook her head. 'Sorry. I'm a bit wound up. I don't think you're an idiot at all. Sorry.'

'It's OK. Why don't you just ring him up, then, and say "I've been sent a picture of you, you worthless shit, marrying some tiara'd bimbo with a spray tan." See if he can sweet talk his way out of that.'

For a moment, Sara was tempted, but then common sense took over.

'No. I need to look him in the eye when I do that. That way I can read his face, too. He's a salesman, Wendy. He's been trained to sell people exactly what they want to hear over the telephone. He's good at that. Pass me the picture again.'

She stared at the partial words on the wall behind the bride. The letters didn't make sense. Wendy squinted across the table, then dragged her mobile, with some difficulty, out of her tight jeans. Idly, Sara noticed that this week, Wendy's manicure was a glowing apricot, with a little sunrise picked out on the ring finger of either hand. Not for the first time, Sara wondered how Wendy ever managed to do anything practical with such astonishing nails, but they seemed to survive, no matter what. She watched with distracted fascination as Wendy opened her phone.

'Hang on. I know that brickwork.'

'What?'

Wendy was frantically rattling through data on her phone, muttering to herself as she scrolled down. 'What the hell is it called?'

'What's what called?'

'If I knew that I wouldn't be looking, would I?' She put her hands to her temples and screwed her eyes shut. 'The funny museum with the shrunken heads and stuff. Twisty pillars.'

'What?'

'In Oxford. That museum. Me and Brian took Tyler and Jade to see the shrunken heads once. Our Jade woke up screaming for a fortnight afterwards. It's not real people,' she added, inconsequentially. 'It's just monkey heads, they think.'

Sara tried to stay focussed. 'The Ashmolean?'

'No, the other one. The quirky one?'

'Pitt Rivers?'

'Yes. That's it, I reckon.' Nails clattering against the screen, Wendy searched through her phone again. 'There. Look.'

Suddenly, VERS

EUM

made sense.

'But surely you can't get married in a museum, Sara? Not back then, anyway. Why's the picture been taken outside the museum?'

Sara stared at the photo, then got up and took her

car keys out of her bag decisively. 'There's only one way to find out, really, isn't there? Fancy a day out?'

Wendy hesitated. 'We could just ring them. It's probably listed on their website.'

'Or we could have a nose around the area.' Sara sensed Wendy's wavering. 'And then we could have lunch out, maybe? My treat.' That swung it, as Sara had known it would. Wendy loved gossipy lunches with her friends.

'OK. I'll just go and lock up next door.'

'Right, you do that. I'll ring work. They can manage without me for the day.'

It was already baking hot when they got into Sara's pale blue BMW. The air-con cut in quickly, but the first couple of minutes were a red-hot hell. June was flaming all right, this year. The forecast had promised 30° or more for the whole week. Reaching Oxford, they stood in the bus shelter at the park-and-ride, trying to find a little shade.

'You do realise this is completely crazy, Sara.'

'So you said before. Several times. I know.' Sara was wrestling with the parking machine, trying to persuade it to accept her registration number. Her tension and Wendy's incessant prattling had made her enter the wrong number twice already. She hoped she wouldn't come back to a parking ticket and a huge fine.

'What are we looking for again?'

'The exact spot where they're standing in the photo.'

'How's that going to help?'

'I've been thinking about that picture. When in doubt, stick with what you know to be facts, and work

10

out the rest from there. This picture was taken in February. That dress is barely held up—strapless, deep plunge—it's not St Lucia, it's Oxford, in February. They can't have got married far from there, or she would've frozen to death. We need to check out all the venues within 500 yards of the place.'

'It's like being on Miss Marple, this isn't it?' Wendy's grin faltered when Sara failed to laugh. She tried again, adopting a more serious tone. 'But the picture was taken 20 years ago.'

'So? That makes it easier for us.'

'How d'you work that out?'

'Fewer places would have had a wedding licence then. Most people still went through the traditional route of church or register office. We ought to be able to track licensed addresses down somehow.'

'Smart thinking, Batman.'

Making an effort, Sara let the corners of her mouth turn up. Wendy subsided into silence as the bus arrived. They sat upstairs, Wendy pointing out all the posh houses, and the contrasting squalid nests that down-and-out people had been forced to make in doorways and derelict buildings. 'That's not right, is it?'

'What?' Lost in her own thoughts, Sara knew she ought to be more grateful of her friend's company, ought to pay her more attention, but it was so difficult to focus.

'Sleeping in doorways like that. In a nice area like this. You'd think they'd make them move on.'

Lost for words at Wendy's lack of compassion for her fellow man, Sara just shook her head. She didn't

11

want to start a row. 'I think this is where we get off.'
They lurched down the stairs as the bus swung into the
bus stop.

At the Pitt Rivers Museum, Sara wasted no time. She
went straight up to the front desk.

'Good morning. I was wondering if it was possible
to get married here?'

The young man stopped tapping at his keyboard and
looked at her blankly.

'This is the Pitt Rivers *Museum*, love.' You were
maybe looking for the registry office? It's not far. I can
give you a map' He started to tear a street map of
Oxford from the pad in front of him. He drew a big
circle with a red pen. 'We're just here, and you need to
wa— '

'No, you misunderstand me. I was wondering
whether you had a wedding licence for the premises?
Can folk get married here?'

He looked bemused.

'I've no idea—nobody has while I've worked here,
but that doesn't mean that you can't, as far as I know.
But let me ring them up in the office. I can find out for
you.'

He beamed at them, pleased to be given something a
little more interesting than his usual run-of-the-mill job,
which seemed largely to involve selling tickets to bus
tours or directing folk to the nearest toilets. Not the
dynamic "Indiana Jones" sort of museum job he'd been
after at all. He explained the situation several times on
the phone, obviously being passed from one person to

another. Eventually he looked up.

'Seems nobody's really sure. We don't think so but if you would give me a few details, I can ring or email you if you like. Nobody can remember a wedding here, but you never know. It might be a golden opportunity for the Pitt Rivers, you know, wedding photos with the dinosaurs, wedding breakfast in the museum café...' He smiled at Sara and Wendy brightly, his PC training kicking in.

'When were you hoping to get married, ladies?' Wendy laughed out loud. Sara went deep pink.

'It's not for us. We're married already—' Realising this didn't sound as she wanted it to either, Sara carried on hastily, 'that is, I'm married, and so is my friend. Not to each other. To men.'

This sounded even worse.

'Although I'm not anti same-sex marriage. Not at all. I'm all for it, in fact...' She was gabbling in her embarrassment. Grinning, Wendy took over.

'What my poor red-faced friend here means, is we're trying to find out whether some people we know got married here? We've got a photo.' She showed the guy 'Graham and Micaela.' He looked at it in fascination, reading the back as well, before handing it back.

'This was taken before I was born. I'm afraid I haven't got a clue.'

They stared at him. Before he was born? But it was barely any time ago at all...1997...Wendy couldn't help herself.

'How old are you?'

The man was affronted.

'I don't see what business it is of yours, but I'm 21 the week after next.'

The women shook their heads in disbelief.

'Come on, Wendy. Thank you,' said Sara turning to the man. 'Happy Birthday.'

As they left the building, Wendy hissed, 'You didn't leave your details…'

'No. This was a ridiculous idea. I should have thought it through more carefully.'

While they were walking down Keble Road, dodging tourists, Sara's phone pinged. A text from Graham.

'Hi sweetheart, can't Skype for a couple of days, off to rural parts w/o net. Love ya loads xxGxx'

'Well, that's probably just as well,' Sara said tightly as she showed Wendy the text. 'To be honest, right now I don't know what I'd say to him. Even if my mouth said the right things, he'd know by my expression that something was wrong.' Wendy didn't reply. Sara could tell that she wouldn't have been so restrained if it had been the other way round, with Brian texting Wendy. He would've got both barrels, no questions asked.

An hour later, sitting in a little noodle bar near the open market, drinking ice-cold orange juice and wishing there was some air-conditioning, Wendy asked, 'Have you still got the envelope the picture came in?'

'Yes, it's probably in the heap on the kitchen table with the rest of the post. I just slung it down when you came in, I think. Why?'

'I wondered if it had an Oxford postmark, whether

the person who sent it was around here somewhere.'

They stared round the bar. Tourists, mainly, caught up in their own lives. None of them looked like a suspect.

'That's an unnerving thought. But they wouldn't know I would come straight here, would they—or that I even know the picture was taken in Oxford?'

'True.' Wendy sucked the last of her orange juice noisily through the paper straw.

'Oh God.' Sara put her hand to her mouth, the colour draining from her face.

'What now?'

'What if they're not here—what if they just sent it to get me out of my house for a while?'

'Why would they do that?'

'I don't know. To do something else while the house was empty. Ransack the place. Burn the house down. Kidnap that wretched cat? We've got to get home.'

'Sara, you're being daft.'

'I know that, but right now I don't care. I've got a very bad feeling about this whole thing. Why wait twenty years before telling me that Graham had another wife? This is someone with an ulterior motive. Blackmail or something. They want to hurt somebody.'

Sara was already on her feet, dropping money on the table, searching through her bag for the bus ticket to get back to Peartree where they had left the car. Shaking her head, Wendy followed her, signing to the girl behind the counter that they'd left money for their food, and waving apologetically, hoping somehow to indicate that a crisis had arisen. The girl crossed swiftly to the table they'd vacated, her concerned expression turning to a smile when she saw the notes Sara had left. She waved thanks at the fat tip

Unwilling to wait for the park and ride bus, Sara commandeered a taxi from under the nose of some American tourists who were just about to get into it. In a cut-glass accent, she said 'I'm so terribly sorry, but we have a tremendous crisis—we have to get home—my husband—' She left the last word hanging in the air, and ever-polite, the American man held the door open for them. 'You take the cab, honey. I hope he's OK.' Wendy heard him say 'She sounded just like Mary Poppins, d'you suppose she's a duchess or something?' to his wife as the taxi pulled away.

The journey home was a bit hairy, to say the least. Sara drove right on the upper edge of the speed limit, taking calculated risks overtaking closely on the bendy road, leaning forwards in her urgency as she drove. Wendy held tightly onto the door handle. They didn't chat. Crunching onto the gravel outside the house, Sara turned to her friend.

'I know I'm being unreasonable, but would you come in with me?'

'OK.'

They went in cautiously, "Hello?"-ing as they went through the rooms, listening for footsteps and watching for danger. Nothing seemed different. Arthur the neighbourhood cat, visiting for the afternoon, wound his fat tabby self round their ankles, meowing and purring, hoping for fuss or food or preferably both. Their empty tea mugs from this morning were still on the kitchen table, and the torn envelope from the photo was in the recycling basket by the back door. Wendy picked it up, opening and shaking it to see if there was anything inside. A bright pink post-it note fluttered onto the table. Sara looked aghast. Wendy turned it over and they read:

'Sara. I thought you might be interested to see this.'

Her hands flew to her mouth.

'They know my first name. This is just too sinister.' The envelope had been addressed to Mrs G Parker.

'Do you want to go to the police? Maybe you should.'

'No. No, they'll arrest him. Bigamy is a crime. He'll go to prison. No.'

Sara sat down heavily, her elbows on the table, rubbing her eyes with the heels of her hands as she tried to make sense of this craziness. She felt sick. Wendy stared at the note again. The lettering was bold, clear and neat.

'Are you quite sure that you don't recognise the handwriting?'

'I'm positive.' Sara's tone was steady once more, her usual control re-established. 'I've been trying to identify it, but I'm certain it isn't anyone I know.'

'Sara, who d'you reckon is the intended victim here?'

'What do you mean?'

'Well, are they trying to get at you, or at Graham?'

'Well, me, obviously. It was sent to me.'

'Yes, but nothing much will happen to you. It's awful, and it's going to change your life. But Graham would lose everything, his job, his wife, his friends—

17

probably his home, even. He's broken the law. He might even go to prison, like you said.' Wendy grimaced and pursed her lips as Sara spoke. Her tone was resigned, flat.

'You mean he might lose his *wives*, Wendy.'

'Yes. I guess so.' She paused, trying another tack. 'I wonder who took the pic? Black and white is unusual for 1997. I wonder if it's a professional photo?' She flicked the picture over again, looking for a photographer's stamp.

'I suppose it might be.' Sara considered the idea. 'But would they have hired a wedding photographer, do you suppose? Surely not? Maybe it was just someone who fancied themselves as arty.'

'True. Got many arty friends?'

Sara laughed wryly. 'Lots. At my work, at Graham's work, people from uni…lots. It was 1997, remember. We didn't have smart phones back then, everyone had a camera instead. Don't you remember? I had a little digital camera with a tiny memory card, thought I was David Bailey.'

'But those friends, the ones who might've taken the picture, they all knew you as a couple?'

'I think so, yes. That's the trouble though, I can't be certain, with Graham working away from home so much. He knows so many people.' She paused. 'People I don't know.'

'Maybe not one of your joint friends, then. What I can't work out though, is why someone would wait twenty years before they decided to send it to you?'

'No. I can't either.'

'Unless?' Wendy stopped, uncertain whether she should voice her concern.

'Unless what?'

'Could it be a previous girlfriend of his? Or a jilted lover, someone like that? An ex-business partner, even? Revenge is best served cold, after all.'

Sara racked her brains. 'I can't remember anyone. We've been together more than twenty-five years.' Tears threatened to overwhelm her. 'What have I ever done to deserve this?'

In a quiet street on the outskirts of Basingstoke, a second batch of envelopes marked 'DO NOT BEND' thudded into a red mailbox. The sender smiled. Job done. This should put the cat well and truly amongst the pigeons.

'What will you do with the photo?'

'At this moment, frankly, I've no idea. I'm not going to put the bloody thing in a silver frame on the mantelpiece, that's for certain.'

'Do you want me to take it home with me? You don't want to stare at this all night, do you? I know you, Sara, you'll worry about it for hours and hours.'

'Yes, take it. No, wait, don't.' She held the hated picture in both hands, her brow creased with indecision. 'Maybe.'

'Would you like to come back home with me and eat with us tonight? So you aren't on your own? Brian's making his famous spagbog.'

Sara shook her head. 'No, but thanks for the offer.

I'd be terrible company, and I've got no appetite anyway.'

'Promise me you'll eat something, though, Sara.'

'I will, yes.'

'Not just a biscuit? You promise?'

'No, not just a biscuit. Thanks for today, Wend. Honestly, I don't know what I'd have done without you.'

They hugged, and Wendy went back home. Would she regale Brian and the kids of today's hideous events? Probably, Sara decided. She locked the back door and got out her laptop. Remembering her promise to Wendy, she opened the fridge door and stared in, hoping for inspiration. Nothing appealed. She cut a chunk off the Brie and stuck it on a plate with a rather sad piece of floppy celery and a couple of crackers. That'd do. Anything on a plate was a meal, wasn't it? Pouring a big glass of wine, she switched on the laptop and started to scour the net. Right. When in doubt, always start with the obvious, she told herself. In the search box, she typed 'Mrs Micaela Parker...'

'Brian? Brian! You'll never guess where I've been all day...' Wendy was surprised to see her husband back home so early. The roofing job must've been easier than he'd led her to believe. He can't have been paid yet though, or he would've been down the Bell for "just a couple of swift ones" with the lads.

Brian grunted from behind his paper.

'Me and Sara went to Oxford—she's had this funny post and it looks like that sleazy toad she's married to has been having it away for YEARS. You know he's always working away from home? I reckon he's got another life, like in that film. She says they Skype every night, but he could be anywhere when he does that, couldn't he? In his car, or outside, anywhere.'

'What are you going on about? How's that got anything to do with Oxford?'

Wendy beamed. For once, she had his attention. 'Make me a cuppa and I'll tell you all about it.'

Bolt from the Blue

Jude bent to grab the post from the fraying doormat. At least this wasn't yet another bill, as far as she could tell. As she picked the letter up, she could feel the summer breeze blowing under the door. She was really going to have to do something about that draught before too long. That was the trouble with living in a house where the front door opened straight into the living room. Last winter she'd had to shove a blanket in front of the gap to catch the howling gale. She stored the thought away with a million other things that she ought to do, and looked at her post.

The envelope was addressed by hand, and although the postmark was blurred she could vaguely see "London Heathrow." Some lucky sod going on their holidays. It was years since she'd had a decent holiday, there was no way could she afford it with three kids, not since Graham had left her high and dry. Hers was the only wage to support the four of them, and the kids always needed something, new shoes, money for a school trip or a birthday party present—two if the twins were invited together. She didn't want them to miss out, but it was tough. Over the years she'd become a demon budgeter, robbing Peter to pay Paul. It wore her down.

The envelope was addressed to Mrs G Parker. Fat chance of that, she thought, pursing her lips. They had never actually got married, just hooked up, and split, and hooked up again and split again. And then that awful phone call had come from Graham's friend, telling her about the accident. She'd been six-and-a-half months pregnant with Robbie and Keira then, and the shock had nearly done for them all. Six weeks' bed rest in hospital, with Poppy, then just two years old, dumped on Granny, Dilys, who managed not to say 'I told you so,' too often.

She ripped open the envelope, mentally writing a shopping list and wondering if she needed to bung some clothes in the washing machine before she went out. Half-interested, she looked down at the glossy picture—a lovely house and a pool, probably somewhere abroad, by the look of the palm trees and the colour of the sky. It could be a holiday advert, perhaps? There was no way this was Weston-super-Mare. A couple were sitting on the edge of the swimming pool, dangling their feet into the water. The woman was in her 50s, pale skinned and slim with an expensive haircut. The diamonds on her left hand twinkled a starburst in the sunlight, as she lifted a glass to her lips. He was smiling, staring into the camera. Jude's heart lurched. It was Graham. What the hell?

She turned the picture over. In neat lettering on the back were the words 'Graham and Sara, Alicante, 2017.'

She couldn't think straight. 2017? But by then Graham had been dead for nearly four years. How could this be true?

There was a wail from the other room.

'Mu-u-m. Robbie bashed me AGAIN. Mum—'

Talk about the true sense of comedy being timing. Jude was not in the mood for this right now. Forgetting her usual patience, she snapped, 'Oh will you lot just shut up? Behave. Just sort yourselves out for once.'

There was a short surprised silence, followed by the sound of a sharp slap. Robbie started to bellow like a factory klaxon. Her head spinning, Jude crashed into the living room like an avenging angel.

'In the garden, all of you, right now.'

'But it's too hot—'

'Now! I need some peace. Five minutes in the fresh air will do you good.'

She opened the back door and the three of them trooped out unwillingly, Keira and Robbie shoving and jostling each other as they always did. Jude breathed deeply and made her voice reasonable.

'Poppy, look after these two for five minutes. I'm just going next door.'

'But, Mum—'

'Five minutes, Poppy.' Her tone brooked no argument.

Next door in number 31, Ruth inhaled deeply on her fake fag. The window and doors were all tightly shut against the day's heat, and the sickly sweet smell of her lemon sherbet vape filled the cluttered room. Upstairs, Ruth's daughter was listening to Spotify at full volume, so loud it made Jude wince. Ruth was completely oblivious to the racket. She held the photograph in both hands and peered at it through the diamanté pound-shop reading glasses that she'd finally unearthed from down the side of the sofa and then perched on the end of her nose.

'So let me get this right, Jude, this guy in the photo is your kids' dad?'

'Yes.'

'Posh.' She nodded approvingly, admiring the even tan and the broad shoulders of the man in the photo.

'Posh and *dead*, Ruth.'

'He don't look so dead to me, babe.' She grinned at Jude and winked lasciviously. The sound of crying from next door grew louder. Jude sighed and got to her feet. Ruth held a hand up, staying her.

'Shaaa-nnon?'

The wailing music upstairs was turned down a fraction, and a disembodied reply came floating down.

'Yeah?'

'Go next door and entertain Jude's kids for a bit, love.'

'Mu-um. Do I have to?'

'Yes. Now.'

Ruth's voice held a touch of steel. The music snapped off, and Jude felt the house shake as Shannon slammed her bedroom door. Begrudging feet stomped down the stairs.

'But they're such miserable little—oh—hi Jude.' Her voice raised half a tone as she tried to backfill the hole she'd just dug for herself.

'Hi Shannon. How are you?'

'I'll just pop next door then.' Blushing, Shannon avoided Jude's eye.

'Thanks, love.' Ruth grinned at Jude. 'Tactful, isn't she?'

'She's right, though. They ARE miserable little—'

'Aren't they all, love? They grow out of it. It might take thirty years, sometimes, but they grow out of it.

Mostly.'

She picked up the picture again.

'So, remind me. What's his name again?'

'Graham.'

'And you thought he was dead?'

'Yes. His friend Mick rang me in the middle of the night when I was expecting the twins. He told me that there had been a pile-up on the M40 and Graham had been killed.'

'And you believed him?'

'Why wouldn't I? You don't ring a total stranger at three in the morning and lie about something like that, do you? I was distraught.'

'What about a funeral?'

'He said he'd ring me with more details as soon as he knew them, but the shock sent me into early labour and I spent almost six weeks in hospital. Poppy had to go and stay with my mum, and by the time the twins were born I reckoned I'd missed the funeral anyway. I was too knackered and too busy to care by then. And I don't do funerals. When you work on an elderly care ward you see enough crying faces without actively seeking them out.'

'Fair enough. And this came in this morning's post?'

'Yeah. It was a complete bolt from the blue. You know when people say their heart was in their mouth?' She touched her throat. 'It was just like that. I'm still shaking, Look.' She held out her hand, as if to prove it, but disappointingly, it remained steady as a rock. ' Well, I feel pretty bloody shaken, anyhow.'

'Bummer. You would. And you're sure it's him?'

'Yes, I'm certain. I was with him for a couple of years, on and off. I KNOW it's him. See that long white scar on his knee there? That's from falling off a motorbike when he was 19. He told me about it once, made me laugh. He was good at making me laugh.' Her mouth, usually smiling, became a thin, bitter line.

'Well, if you want my expert medical opinion, I'd say it looks like he's not dead then.'

'Hmmm. Funnily enough, I'd come to that very same conclusion too.'

'Still alive, but just proved to be a bit of a shit, I'd say.'

'I think you could be right.'

The women were quiet for a moment, weighing up the constant duplicity of men.

'Seems to me you're better off without a low-life like that. I'd offer you a gin but there's none left. Fancy a brew? There might even be a Jaffa Cake or two, if Shannon hasn't scoffed them all.'

The sound of giggling floated in from the garden. Jude forced herself to calm down. A cup of tea would give her a breathing space. The ache that encircled her head loosened its grip a little. 'Go on then.'

Mistaken Identity

The envelope was addressed by hand. Martha picked it up out of the wire cage that hung behind her letterbox, together with a get-two-for-the-price-of-one advert from 'SuperChick', another one from 'Specs-You-Like' and a postcard of the Eiffel Tower, addressed to Doreen next door, that had been put through by accident. She smiled; it was a rare treat to get a hand-written piece of post these days, she thought. But disappointingly, there was no letter inside; the envelope contained only a photograph—a picture of three young children in a playground somewhere—two little girls and a small boy, mixed race and laughing, and a slim black woman who was pushing one of the girls on a swing.

Puzzled, Martha turned the picture over. A typed label on the back said 'Poppy, Robbie and Keira Parker, May 2017'. She stared at it, bemused. She didn't know who the children were, or why someone would send her the picture. A handsome family though, whoever they were. Dismissing it as mistaken identity, she left all the post on the hall table, and went upstairs. Just as she got to the top of the stairs, the doorbell rang. Martha tutted and trudged back down.

'Morning, Mrs Parker. How are we today?'

'I don't know about you, Janet, but I'm too hot and my knees hurt.'

'Oh dear, never mind.'

Janet never listened to a word she said, but she was a

ferociously good cleaner, so Martha put up with her. One of these days she'd give her a key of her own, she thought. Save all this to-ing and fro-ing on the stairs. She could surely trust her with a key after all this time.

'The usual, today, Mrs P? Anything special you want me to do?'

'Just the usual, please Janet. And could you empty the washing machine, and peg the things out? We may as well put the heat wave to good use.'

'Right you are.'

Janet took off her completely unnecessary bulky blue cardigan and draped it over the back of one of the upright chairs in the hallway. Underneath, she wore the kind of check nylon overall that had vanished from the shops in the 1970s. Martha had always wondered where she had bought such a museum exhibit. No self-respecting dust or grime would be seen anywhere near Janet. She attacked mess and dirt as though it had personally offended her. Martha suspected that she had undiagnosed OCD, and was putting it to good use. The house always sparkled when Janet had been.

On the stroke of eleven, Janet and Martha drank coffee, a habit they'd evolved over the last fifteen years. Janet would tell Martha all about her lovely boys in Australia and their no-good wives, and her amazingly gifted grandchildren, and Martha would smile and nod, filling the appropriate gaps with suitably shocked or impressed noises, as the occasion demanded.

Today, the photograph from this morning's post was on the kitchen table.

'I didn't think you'd want me to throw this away,

Mrs P. Your grandkids, are they?'

Martha braced herself. That was the trouble with getting friendly with people who worked for you, they thought they had the right to know everything about you. She could see that Janet was intrigued. Martha hadn't spoken about Graham to Janet, although she'd never denied that he existed. Of course, there was never any evidence of him at Christmas, or on her birthday either. Janet must've read the label on the back of the picture, Martha realised. These children were called Parker. She must've put two and two together and made five.

'I've no idea who they are. The photo arrived out of nowhere this morning. No note, nothing. Someone has undoubtedly made a mistake. They've got the wrong Mrs Parker, I think.'

'I'll put it in the bin, then, shall I?'

'I'll do it.'

'Right you are.'

She saw Janet smile to herself, no doubt convinced that she wasn't telling the truth. She probably thought that Martha was being a silly, racist old woman, that she'd lost touch with her son—her only, precious son, just because his wife was black. As if that would matter.

Martha didn't know why she hadn't let Janet throw the picture away. As the vacuum rumbled in the sitting room, she picked the photo up again and stared at the little family. It genuinely hadn't occurred to her that they might be related to her. Maybe Graham had got married to this slender girl, with the lovely laughing face, and they had produced these three happy children.

She almost hoped it was the truth. Their skin was lighter than their mother's, their father might be white. Who knew? Who cared? She wondered whether the two little ones were twins, and which little girl was Poppy and which Keira. The boy, Robbie, looked full of mischief, much as Graham had at that sort of age.

Martha fetched her reading glasses. Was there a resemblance? Maybe all small boys had that expression when they were having fun. Later, maybe, when Janet had gone home, she would brave that damned ladder and dig out all the old photograph albums from the loft—just to see if she could find a picture of Graham as a little boy, just to see. No reason, really. Idle curiosity, that's all.

Martha positioned the picture carefully back exactly where Janet had left it. No point in fuelling her vivid imagination, after all.

Una Aguja en el Pajar

The sound of the garden gate alerted Sara that she was about to be disturbed. She yawned and stretched, her spine complaining from long hours spent over a keyboard. She was due for a break. Wendy tapped on Sara's kitchen window, as she passed it on her way to the back door, as she usually did. Sara, looking up from the polished oak table where she was typing on her laptop, waved 'hi' and beckoned her in.

'Morning, Wendy.'

'Hi. How are you doing this fine sunny morning?' She peered at her friend. Sara, though smiling, was pale, and there were dark smudges under her eyes. ' For Chrissakes, Sara. Have you even been to bed?'

'Oh, I grabbed a couple of hours on the sofa. I'm absolutely fine.' She ignored the exasperated look that Wendy threw at her.

'Have you heard anything from Graham yet?'

'No, that text said he's incommunicado for a few days. Remember?'

'Oh yeah. So, how are you really?'

'Fine.' Sara was dismissive. She didn't quite meet Wendy's eyes.

'Did you find anything?' Wendy nodded at the laptop enquiringly.

'Not really.' Sara tried to keep the note of complacency out of her voice but failed spectacularly.

'Which means you might have found something?'

'Maybe.'

'What then?'

'I couldn't find anything for Micaela Parker. Well I could, but it wasn't this woman.' She flicked a finger at the photo, which looked smudged and dog-eared, as though it had been handled rather a lot since yesterday afternoon. 'So then, I looked up Graham instead; you know the sort of listings I mean, accounts, company reports and business details. Directors lists, that kind of thing?'

Wendy nodded knowledgeably. She didn't have a clue about the lists, but she wanted to keep Sara talking.

'And I went back year upon year. In 1996 one Micaela Fernandez joined the company as the regional representative in Valencia.'

'Graham works in Spain a lot, doesn't he?'

'He certainly does. Do you want to see a picture of Senorita Micaela Fernandez?'

'I don't know. Do I?'

'You bet you do. Here you are.' She turned the screen round. Dressed in a work suit and with her hair scraped into a more business-like bun, the serious dark woman on the screen was still, undoubtedly, the glamorous bride from the wedding photo.

'Oh Christ.'

'Uh-huh. I thought something remarkably similar. Possibly something quite a lot ruder, though. Micaela Fernandez is in the company report again in 1997, and then she vanishes.'

'Could you find her again anywhere else?'

'Do you know how many Micaela Fernandez-es there are in Spain? Hundreds. Possibly thousands. It's like looking for a needle in a haystack, or "una aguja en el pajar", as I looked up in a quiet moment at about half past three this morning.'

'Oh.'

Wendy looked at Sara. Yesterday's troubled woman had vanished. This woman in front of her burned with determination. There was an iron core down her spine that held her bolt upright, even though she was clearly knackered from a night without sleep. Ever practical, Wendy tucked a stray strand of red hair behind her ear, switched on the kettle and shoved some bread in the Dualit toaster. Her kitchen was nowhere near as nice as this one. Wendy ran a finger enviously across the bespoke cabinet edge. Smooth and curved, the wood begged to be caressed. Wendy pushed the envy away. If they'd had oak work surface like this in her kitchen, it'd soon be covered in white rings from mugs and cans. She was better off with the sparkly laminate they'd chosen. Behind her, Sara continued to tap. Pulling the laptop gently away from her friend, Wendy filled the ensuing space with a mug of tea and a plate of toast and jam.

'But I was just about to start searching for—'

'Shut up, Sara. Eat. I bet you didn't eat last night did you? Eat.' Wendy knew she was being bossy, possibly even overstepping the mark, but Sara looked tired and pale. On the draining board sat a plate with a dried up chunk of cheese and a browning stick of celery. Arthur, wandering past Sara's house on the off chance, jumped onto the kitchen windowsill and looked at the cheese hungrily. He miaowed silently through the glass, but

Wendy flapped a tea towel at him. The cat belonged to everybody and nobody, and ate, it was generally reckoned, about fifteen meals a day. He gave her a look of disgust and jumped down again, to go and try his luck elsewhere.

Sara looked at her friend ruefully, and bit into the toast obediently. She looked surprised how hungry she was.

'I had no appetite at all last night. This morning, I'm ravenous.'

Wendy sipped her tea and waited. 'So, have you decided what you're going to do yet?'

Sara shook her head, chewing in a determined way to finish her mouthful and talk again quickly. Swallowing hard, she said, 'No, not yet. I've decided to play it cool. Assemble my troops before I take them to battle, as it were.' She picked up the mug.

Wendy nodded encouragingly. 'That's probably a good move.'

'Yes. And I can't really ring work and tell them I'm not going to make it in again. I rang yesterday morning and said I wouldn't be in for a couple of days because I'd had some bad family news, that's bought me a bit of space, but I really have to go back in tomorrow, just to sort a few cases out and see how everyone is coping. That's the trouble with being the boss, you can't have a duvet day when the shit hits the fan.'

'Are you sure you're OK to go back? You look really knackered.'

Sara grinned wryly at her bluntly-spoken friend. 'Thanks very much. Of course I'm OK. I'm not ill.

Nobody has died. I've just discovered my marriage is a total sham, that's all. It's hardly life threatening. Lots of women discover exactly the same thing every day. It's depressingly ordinary.'

'I suppose so. Not everyone finds out that they've been fooled for the past 20 years though.'

'I might not have been. They might not still be together. We don't know for sure, do we?'

'Well, no, but—'

'But nothing. We're imagining the worst-case scenario. It might just have been a fling.'

'They got married, Sara.' Wendy sipped her tea and avoided Sara's face. She braced herself for the backlash, but nothing happened. Sara took a deep breath, as though making a decision to tell her a secret.

'Yes, but I was thinking about that. How? How could they get married? Banns are read. Checks are made. You have to give twenty-eight days notice of getting married. I looked it up. Twenty-eight days, while they check you aren't a double-crossing lying cheating pernicious bastard with a frightened young wife who's stuck in hospital, being pumped full of hormones and IVF drugs trying to conceive your baby.'

Wendy refused to be put off. 'So how come there's a wedding picture?'

Sara spun the laptop back towards her.

'I considered that too. So I started to research, "obstacles to marriage" instead. Then I discovered this...'

She brought up a page on her laptop about humanist weddings, and turned the screen again so that Wendy could read it. She had highlighted one sentence. 'Our humanistic weddings do not currently have legal status.'

'It suddenly occurred to me that if this Micaela Fernandez didn't speak fluent, colloquial English, she might not have realised it wasn't a legal wedding. She might not even have had any idea of what English weddings are normally like, and Graham can be very convincing when he tries. I reckon that's what he persuaded her to do. You can get "married" anywhere in a humanistic wedding, from what I read. In a wood, by the sea, in your own front room, if you want. It's just a public commitment of your feelings for each other. It's not legal until you sign something, and you can only do that at a proper wedding, with a recognised, registered person conducting the ceremony.'

'So are there any records anywhere?'

'I doubt it very much.'

'Blimey.'

Sara sat back, triumphant in her sleuthing. Her chin came up, and her eyes seemed brighter. Wendy imagined she could hear the cogs turning in Sara's mind.

'What do we do now, then, Sara?'

'I have no idea. Try to find out if they're still together, I suppose.'

'How?'

Sara shook her head, sighing. She frowned again. 'I was rather hoping you might have a bright idea about that, Wendy. You're the one who wanted to be Miss Marple.'

Verbal Minefields

It had just gone 7am. Jude fastened her seatbelt and looked in the rear view mirror to check her kids had done the same. She was already fairly knackered, and she'd a busy shift ahead, they were understaffed, as ever. She hadn't really slept last night, wondering about Graham. If he was alive, why did he pretend to have been in an accident? How come he hadn't been in contact? Vaguely, she was aware that a question was being repeated.

'Sorry?'

'You weren't listening. You never listen to me.' Seven-and-a-half and going on fourteen. Jude sighed.

'I'm sorry, Poppy. I was miles away. What did you say?'

'It doesn't matter.' Poppy folded her arms, stuck out her bottom lip and stared out of the window mutinously.

'It does matter. Tell me.'

'Poppy said—' There was mischief in Robbie's tone. Jude braced herself for the inevitable bickering.

'Shut up, Robbie.' Poppy's tone was the long-suffering sound of a sophisticated girl plagued with an infuriating younger brother.

'Poppy?' Silence. Waiting for the lights to change, Jude tried again. She glanced over her shoulder. 'Poppy, will you please tell me what you said before. I'm sorry I wasn't listening then. I'm listening now and I want to hear whatever it was that you wanted to tell me.'

If parenting ever went out of fashion, just think how the diplomatic service would be flooded with experienced applicants, Jude thought.

'It doesn't matter.'

'Poppy.' It was a warning tone. The car behind her beeped as the light went to green. She slammed the Panda in gear and the car lurched in her haste.

'Richard said that we didn't have a daddy and so we were all bastards. What's a bastard?' The sentence came out all in one breath. Poppy knew this was a dangerous word, even if she didn't understand its true meaning.

'What the—? Who the hell is Richard?' The traffic was already snarling up. Today was getting better and better.

'He's a boy in my class.'

'He sounds a real charmer.' Jude aimed for a calm tone of voice. 'You do have a daddy, love, but he went away.'

'Why? Didn't he love us?'

'Of course he did. But sometimes things like that happen.'

'Why?'

'I don't know, Poppy.' Jude turned off the main road with relief and pulled up at the kerbside, not too far from her mother's house. She put the handbrake on and fixed a careless smile on her face. 'Here we are, then. Grannie will be waiting for you.'

'Mum am I a bar stud too?'

'No, Robbie, you aren't. It's not a nice word. Please don't say it again. You might make Grannie Dil cry.'

This was the ultimate threat. Jude hoped to God it

worked. Life was hard enough without her mother going on about the bad language her grandkids used, and where they might have picked it up. Jude's mum was a firm believer in an apple not falling far from the tree, and Jude's own guilt levels were set to maximum as it was. Juggling reading bags and lunchboxes, she hustled the kids inside, and planted a smacking kiss on her mum's cheek. 'I don't know what I'd do without you.'

Dilys sighed. 'And what about my retirement plans, that's what I'd like to know.'

'They keep you young, Mum.'

'They'll put me in an early grave, that's what they'll do. Some of the things that boy comes out with—'

Jude lowered her voice. 'He's coming out with a few choice things this morning. Some delightful kid at school told Poppy she was a bastard yesterday.'

Her mother's hands flew to her mouth and her eyes widened with shock. 'Oh my Lord.'

'Mmm. So I hope I've damped that one down a bit, but brace yourself.'

She kissed the children. 'Be good for Grannie Dilys, kids. See you at six. Thanks, Mum. They've all got their lunchboxes and their reading bags are just by the front door.'

Jude pulled out into the traffic, glancing at her watch as she did so. Traffic was always busy on the way to the hospital. She sincerely hoped that there was still some parking left. Her shift started at eight, and the car park could be a nightmare.

Back in the immaculately clean, if slightly battered,

kitchen at Grannie Dilys's house, wide-eyed and supremely innocent, his budding horns barely visible through his curls, Robbie asked, 'Grannie, what's a bar stud?'

Retro-chic or a Tough Old Bag?

In her spare room, Martha surveyed the loft ladder with hatred. All those TV hospital programmes told you not to climb ladders once you hit sixty. In fact, Martha had hit sixty running, and at seventy had taken up Pilates, but now, at seventy-five, she wondered whether she had the strength to get up the ladder, and more importantly, if she could get out of the loft again safely once she got in.

Carefully moving the pictures from the wall nearest to where the ladder would descend, she sighed, wondering if this was such a good idea after all. She stood for a long moment, gazing at the photograph of her late husband. 'I'm being a silly old woman, aren't I?' she asked him. 'I know what you'd say. You'd say, "Would you like me to do that for you, my love?" You never questioned anything I did or said.' Briefly holding Bernard's photo to her heart, she put it gently in the centre of the floral bedspread and turned resolutely back to the task ahead.

Taking the long hooked pole in both hands, Martha tried to open the hatch, and was surprised how long it took her to catch hold of the little hoop at the end of the ladder to pull it down into the room. It was nearly as difficult as threading a needle, and Martha found that tipping her head back for so long while she tried to hook the wretched thing made her feel a bit giddy. Eventually she managed, and pulled as hard as she could. The heavy ladder came rattling down much faster than she was prepared for, wrenching her wrist as it did so. Martha dropped the pole and swore fiercely. Her arm really hurt. It even hurt to touch it, and it started to swell immediately. Her stomach churning with the sudden pain, she sat heavily on the end of the spare bed, with tears of pain and frustration in her eyes. She hated the idea that she was getting old. She had a sudden thought and tried to get her rings off her fingers, but they had already swollen too much for that. Years of playground duty supervising small children told her not to bother trying to get a doctor's appointment. She gathered her wits and, biting her lip against the pain, went carefully downstairs, one step at a time, to ring for a taxi.

'I'm sorry, love,' said the woman on the call desk. 'I haven't got a car for an hour. There's a big funeral in town and they're all booked out.' The second firm said the same thing.

Damn. She didn't like to do it, but she rang emergency services. The dispatcher was sympathetic but practical. 'You've done the right thing.' A first responder was in the area, and would be with her shortly. She unlocked the front door as instructed and left it on the latch. "Shortly" could mean anything up to an hour, she supposed. Waiting for anything frustrated her. She'd always been the same, fuming in slow queues, filling in words for people when the spoke too slowly. It was only when she was with children that she could be patient, waiting forever while they spelled out a word phonetically from the latest reading book, or nodding in encouragement when they struggled with division, counting on their fingers while they tried to work a knotty sum out. Adults, though, were a different matter. She paced the hall a little, noticing that Janet had missed a cobweb inside the bowl of the uplighter, then decided she would be better waiting in the kitchen, where she could at least rest her arm on the table.

Janet, eco-friendly as ever, had left the kettle just full enough for her next drink, with a cup and saucer placed on a tray next to the coffee jar. Martha decided a hot sweet drink would do her good while she waited. She flipped the switch on.

Damn whoever had sent that picture. She was being a silly old woman, thinking they were Graham's children. She was clutching at straws. She hadn't seen Graham in nearly twenty-eight years, not since the big row at his father's funeral. Even if he did have children, they would probably be in their teens at least by now, not as young as the three on the photograph. She might well be a grandmother, or even a great-grandmother, she thought with alarm. She might never find out.

The kettle clicked itself off. Distracted by memories and forgetting her injury, she picked it up with her right hand, yelling with the sudden pain in her wrist. She dropped the kettle and the lid came open, sending a short cascade of boiling water across the work surface and down the cupboard door, splashing her legs and feet. The combined shock and pain was too much, and she stepped back too quickly, slipping on the wet floor, and hitting her head on the corner of the table with a bang.

At the front door, the first responder rang the bell.

Getting no answer, he tried the door handle, and finding it unlocked, stepped inside the house. 'Hello?' he called. 'Mrs Parker? Martha? It's the ambulance service? Hello?'

He walked down the hall, checking the rooms on either side, until he reached the kitchen. Martha was sitting slumped against the kitchen cupboard, groggy and bleeding. The floor around her was shiny and wet. Deciding there was too much fluid for it to be a toilet accident, he cast his eye around and spotted the kettle on its side, and the flooded worktop. The old lady's legs and one foot were blotchy and pink.

'Hello, m'dear, can you tell me your name? I'm Pete, I'm the first responder from the ambulance. You look like you've been in the wars, m'dear. Can you remember what happened?'

Martha nodded and then groaned. 'Martha. Martha Parker.' Everything seemed to have a red sheen and her face was sticky. She raised her good hand to her eyes.

'I think you've bumped your head a bit, Martha. Hang on.'

He opened his bag, and put a wad of gauze gently where she'd split her eyebrow.

'You're going to have a lovely shiner there. They'll just tape it up though, I doubt you'll even need a stitch. Nothing to worry about.' His voice was calm and reassuring. 'Can you tell me what happened?'

As best as she could, Martha tried to explain. The first responder was wrapping her scalded legs in cling film and the pain was subsiding a little, but her wrist hurt like hell. He pulled out his radio. 'A bang on the head needs checking out down at the Royal, Martha. I'm going to get you some transport.' Checking her over, he helped her off the floor and onto one of the kitchen chairs, talking to her calmly about the weather and other inconsequential matters while his eyes registered her every reaction. Eventually, there was another knock at the door. Despite her protestations, Martha was soon loaded onto a stretcher and wheeled out.

'A head injury, a suspected broken wrist and a few fairly nasty scalds, Mrs Parker,' said the ambulance man. 'I'd make the most of the ride if I were you. We're going to take you to Gloucester Royal. Is there anyone we can ring for you? Family, friends, a neighbour?'

'No. Nobody. Thank you.'

Never one to take more than a reluctant Paracetamol, the unfamiliar painkillers they had given her were making Martha drowsy. She closed her eyes, sensing rather than seeing her neighbour's curtains twitching. This'd give the old dears something to talk about. Great.

At the hospital she went straight through to Resus, one of the plus points of old age, she thought wryly to herself. An X-ray revealed her to have broken her wrist.

'But I didn't fall or anything. Not then anyway.' She said indignantly. 'The ladder came down a bit fast, that's all. It's ridiculous that I've broken a bone through a silly thing like that.'

'It's easily done, love. You're facing an op, I'm afraid; they'll need to put a plate in there to help it heal.' The nurse, her blue dress straining against her curves, had a slightly dismissive air, though her voice was kind. Martha was aware of thinking "Why doesn't she just wear the next size up?" She forced herself to concentrate.

'Can I go home?'

'Is there anyone there to keep an eye on you? You had a nasty bump and we're concerned about possible concussion.'

Martha hesitated.

'My neighbour is very good.'

'What about your son?' The nurse was reading Martha's next of kin on the form.

'No.' Martha's tone was sharp.

'Has he been contacted for you?'

'No. No thank you. No need to concern him.'

'Well, OK, we'll try and find you a bed for the night here, I think. Just to be on the safe side. Or we can see if there is a convalescent bed in a nursing home, if you prefer?'

'Dear God, no, not some rabbit hutch full of old folk dribbling and snoring and going gaga all over the place? Over my dead body.'

The nurse half smiled. 'If you're sure.'

'I am.' Martha was indignant. 'I'm perfectly able to look after myself, thank you.'

'Of course.'

Martha sat on the edge of the bed, fuming and cursing silently in her head. This was such a ridiculous waste of time and resources. She would be fine on her own. She would just sign something and discharge herself. Looking around for her handbag, she got rapidly to her feet. The world suddenly tilted violently, and she realised to her horror that she was going to vomit. A tall porter bringing a wheelchair in pushed the curtain to one side just at the wrong moment.

'Here we go, Mrs Parker, your chariot awaits. Oh whoops—'

He spun the chair out of the way just in time and caught her as she crumpled.

'Can I get some help in here please?' he called through to the next cubicle. 'Just you sit back, love.' He steered her back towards the bed, holding her shoulders to help her keep her balance. The vertigo was overwhelming. Someone lifted her legs up onto the bed and she lay back against the pillow feeling exhausted and tearful.

'I'm so sorry.' Martha was mortified. She felt too weak to open her eyes. 'So sorry.'

'Don't you worry, my dear, worse things happen, I can tell you.'

A disembodied voice sent instructions for a cleaner, and Martha felt cool firm hands checking her pulse.

'We're going to admit you, Martha. OK?'

She nodded feebly, eyes still shut. A plastic cup was held to her lips.

'Have a little sip of this. It's only water, but it'll make you feel a bit better.'

'Thank you.'

The journey up to the ward made her feel worse, lying on a trolley bed being whisked down corridors and up in the lift. The ceiling tiles sped past at a rate of knots. She closed her eyes, battling the motion sickness.

'Nearly there.'

Her bed was turned into a ward and backed into a space, where the brakes were put on with a thud.

'There you go. This is Jude. She'll look after you.'

The latest nurse bustled around, asking exactly the same questions that Martha had answered downstairs already, taking yet more of what Martha knew would be identical vital readings. She knew that everywhere you go in hospital they take exactly the same information from you, your name your age your blood pressure. It was getting on Martha's nerves.

'How long will I be stuck in here?'

The nurse smiled and gave a little shrug.

'Well now you're here, we'll see if we can hustle through getting your wrist fixed. Two birds with one stone, eh, and we can treat your scalds more effectively as well. A couple of days, maybe? You should be home by the end of the week, I reckon.'

Martha fretted.

'The milk will stack up on the doorstep. I'll get burgled.'

'I'm sure that won't happen.'

'Yes, it will. You see it on the TV all the time. They watch for things like that, burglars. They come and knock on the door of empty houses. Call, and shout, peer through windows, they're bold as brass. They'll ransack the place. I'll have to go home.' She tried to sit up.

'Martha, no.' The nurse was firm. 'You stay right there. I'll sort it. What about your next door neighbours? Would they put out a note for the

49

milkman?'

'Well, possibly, but—'

'Do you have their phone number?'

'It's in a little book in my handbag.' Martha twisted round to look. 'Do you know what happened to my bag—I had it when I came in—it's got my keys and everything in it?' She could hear herself, her voice sounded old and anxious.

Jude rummaged in the locker, pulling out an old-fashioned brown leather bag with a shiny gold twist clasp.

'Here you go. That's a very smart bag, Martha.'

'It was my mother's. I suppose that they would call it vintage, now, wouldn't they? Or retro-chic, isn't that the phrase? It's just a tough old bag, like me.'

If she had expected a polite smile and a response to the negative, Martha was mistaken. Jude roared with laughter.

'Excellent. You stay being a tough old bag if you want, Martha. Feisty women are the most powerful. You should meet my mother, she rules my kids with a fierceness that would put Genghis Khan in the shade.'

She grinned and Martha found herself smiling back.

'How many children have you got?'

'Three. Two girls and a boy.'

'You look far too young. Mind you, these days, everyone under fifty looks young to me. It's true what they say, you know, as you get older, all the policemen look like schoolboys.'

'You're too kind. Can I look in your bag for you, Martha? Is it a diary or something with the phone number in?'

'I'll do it myself, thank you.'

'Of course.' Jude twisted the catch open for her and passed the bag across with a smile. Martha balanced her reading glasses with a little difficulty on her sore face, and flicked through her little red notebook with one hand. She indicated a name on the page and passed the book over.

'There. Doreen Knight. She lives next door. Do you mind ringing her?'

'No, it's absolutely fine. I'll get the ward clerk to do it right now.'

She took the book, opened the blue papery curtains around Martha's bed and strode off towards the desk.

Martha looked around the ward. It was just as she had feared. There were three other beds in the bay. In the bed opposite, an ancient human of indeterminate sex lay as pale and still as a corpse, eyes shut, toothless mouth open, snoring gently. The sign above the bed gave lifting and turning instructions. In the bed by the window, an old lady in a hospital gown was staring blankly out at the sky, singing to herself in a high, reedy voice. The knobbles of her spine jutted through the thin cotton gown as though they were going to push right through it, and she rocked gently forward and back while she sang. In the bed next to Martha's own, an avid-eyed woman, again thin to the point of skeletal, looked at her eagerly, delighted to have some new stimulation.

'Ooh, 'ello love. What you in for then?' Inwardly, Martha sighed. She considered pretending to be

German, or Spanish, or anything non-English speaking, but reasoned without the woman's nosiness.

'Martha, is it? I heard that nurse say it. Jude, that's her name. She's all right but they're not really interested in us, are they? Bed blockers, that's what we are. Too old and knackered to cope by ourselves and not ill enough to worry about. I'm Gloria.' She held out a claw for Martha to shake. Martha hesitated, then started to lift her left hand awkwardly.

'Oh dear, 'urt your wrist?'

Gloria eyed the temporary plaster, clambering out of her own bed and coming to sit on the chair next to Martha's. She offered up a battered and greying paper bag half-full of toffees and empty wrappers.

'D'you want one of these? They're really nice. My daughter brought them in yesterday. I could unwrap one for you if you like. Pop it in for you. No trouble.' She started to untwist a sweet.

'No—' Gloria's nails were chipped and grimy. 'No, thank you. Not a toffee.'

'Not got your own gnashers any more, love?' Gloria cackled.

'Mmm.' It wasn't true, but it was the easiest thing to say.

'I'm in for me old trouble. You know, down there.' Gloria gave her a knowing look. Everything has gone south. I feel like I've got a pudding in my—'

'Gloria, shouldn't you be putting your feet up?'

Never had an interruption been so welcome.

Jude was back, putting the little book in Martha's left hand as she deftly steered Gloria away. Martha shot her a grateful look.

'Martha needs to get some sleep. She's got concussion and she needs a bit of peace, so I'm going to draw this curtain, all right? You can chat later.'

Gloria muttered something about 'only being friendly, welcoming the new girl, being a good neighbour.' Jude put her head through the curtain.

'We managed to speak to your next-door neighbour. She'll stop the milk and keep an eye on the place for you. She hopes you feel better soon. OK?'

'Thanks very much.'

'Would you like a cup of tea?' Martha nodded, gratefully. 'Did you have anything to eat today?'

'Oh yes. Breakfast. And a cup of coffee earlier.'

'It's nearly three o'clock. I'll find you a couple of biscuits to go with the tea, shall I?'

At quarter to six, Jude started her handover. All the patients were fed and sorted, ready for the night shift. Karen, one of the bank night nurses, was in a bad mood.

'Any difficult ones? She asked. 'I'm just not putting up with any BS tonight. Is that Vera still here?'

'No, she's gone back to Green Hedges.'

'Thank God for that. Miserable cow.' Sometimes, Jude wondered why Karen had gone in for nursing. It couldn't be the fabulous money or the sociable hours, and she always seemed to resent being here.

'This is Martha. She was admitted this afternoon, after an accident at home. She's got minor burns on her legs and left foot, and she is waiting to get her right wrist plated. Mild concussion.' She listed the drugs

Martha had been prescribed. Karen caught Martha's eye and nodded.

'Evening.'

'Good evening.' Martha sounded like a stuck-up teacher that Karen had once had. A right old dragon, she'd been. Karen checked the paperwork and looked up sharply as she read the patient's full name. 'Did you used to teach, Martha? You sound like a teacher.'

To her surprise, Martha nodded. 'I did, and I remember your face. You're Karen Watkiss'

'Wow. Yes. Karen Benton now.'

Martha smiled slightly. 'You were a clever child. Always sorting your friends out, as I remember. It's nice to see you've done something worthwhile with your life.'

'Yes, well, thank you, Mrs Parker.'

Suddenly Karen was nine years old again.

'Martha.'

'Martha. Thanks. See you later.'

Flustered, she indicated to Jude they should move onto the next bed. Jude was grinning broadly.

'Thank you, Mrs Parker,' she mimicked in a sing-song, sotto voce.

'Oh shut up. Force of habit, that's all. She was a right dragon.'

From behind the curtain, Martha's amused voice drifted across.

'I still am, dear. I still am.'

Costa del Cheat

The pub garden was crowded, and the children on the bouncy castle were screaming, probably with delight, but it was difficult to tell. Sara and Wendy had managed to grab the last free table, a wobbling ornate black metal one that everyone else had rejected in favour of the sturdier wooden picnic tables. Wendy was fiddling with the edge of the cardboard beermat, separating it into layers with her perfect apricot nails. 'Sara, I had this thought.'

'Oh yes?' Sara was watching the children. She wondered for a moment whether she would have been a good mother, and then battened her imagination and her emotions down tightly again. Thinking like that got you nowhere. She sat up a little straighter and sipped her drink, pulling her focus back to her friend. 'What?'

'That villa where you and Graham stay in Spain every year?'

Every year for the last five, Sara and Graham had holidayed in Calpe, at Graham's friend Mick's villa. Graham always played golf all day, leaving at first light before it got too hot, and returning as the sun was going down. He had a handicap of six, he said. Apparently that was good. Disinterested in golf, Sara lay in the sun, working on her tan, reading trashy novels and vaguely missing the banter at work. In the evenings they went to the local Bodega, where Graham was received with open arms and much backslapping, whilst Sara was nodded at politely and called Senõra. Once, she asked Graham how they knew him so well.

'We play golf together quite often.' It had seemed a good enough answer at the time.

'Casa Nuevo? What about it?'

'Well, I remembered you saying that Graham borrowed it from a friend of his.'

'Yes, that's right. Why? Were you thinking of going to Spain this year?'

Wendy shook her head. 'No. Who?'

'What?'

'Who did you borrow if from? What's the friend's name?'

'It's one of Graham's ex-colleagues called Mick something. I never actually met him. Graham used to sort out all the arrangements. He's set up on his own, now, I think.' Sara was puzzled where this conversation was going.

'Right.' More shredding of the beermat.

Sara gave her a hard look. 'Spit it out.'

Wendy looked awkward. 'What's Mick short for?'

'Mich-ael.' Sara spoke as though Wendy was being particularly stupid. Then she paused.

Wendy looked at her, her face emotionless. 'Or?'

'Shit. I'm such a fool. Or Micaela. Of course.' She shook her head at her own gullibility.

'It might not be. It was just a thought—you know—one of those stupid three o'clock ones that disturbs your dreams. It might not be anything like that. It was just a thought.' She looked away, unhappy that she'd even mentioned it.

'Of course it must be Micaela. He probably calls her

Mick. He must've been really pleased with that one.'

'But if it's her house, why would he take you there? What if one of the neighbours started talking to you? Wouldn't he be worried that they'd let the cat out of the bag?'

'They're Spanish. They mostly don't speak English much beyond "Hello" and "lovely day". Graham does all the talking when we're in Spain so I've no need to speak the language. I can ask for the bill, or for more wine, or the directions to the loo. It's enough.'

Wendy winced. She'd clearly thought Sara was cleverer than that.

'It's lazy, I know, but I never saw the need to learn. If we go to France, I speak French, and Graham says nothing. If we go to Spain, Graham speaks Spanish, and I keep quiet. Division of labour, you know. Maybe Micaela's in on the joke. Maybe she stays around when we go over. Oh my God. He says he plays golf all day. I either lie by the pool or take myself off to the beach, or into Alicante, or something. "You enjoy yourself," he says. "Indulge yourself. Get some me time." Suppose he's not playing golf? Suppose he's with her somewhere? I feel sick.' She reached for her glass, but it was empty.

Wendy pushed her own gin and tonic towards her friend. 'Here—your need is greater than mine. Have a sip of this.'

Sara slugged the drink in one and banged the glass down onto the wrought iron table, which wobbled even more precariously. Wendy crinkled her brow as if she feared for the glass.

'I need to have this out with him right now. This has gone far enough.' As if on cue, Sara's phone beeped. It was another text.

> *'Hi sweetie. Off to catch flight to L.A. Big merger meeting. Not sure when I'll be free. Will text you later. Kisses. xxGxx.'*

Wendy took the phone out of Sara's hands, as she started to type fiercely.

'Hang on, hang on, what about all that stuff about getting your troops assembled before you went to war? Give it an hour before you get back to him.'

'Why? I want some truths from the lying bastard.'

'Of course you do, but he's going to have days to concoct a story and write the perfect text message if you confront him now, isn't he? Much better to wait until you're face-to-face.'

Sara could see the logic in her friend's argument.

'OK, but I need to do something positive. I refuse to just sit here while he's with her.'

'You don't know that he's with her.'

For once Wendy was in charge. It was a strange reversal. Sara felt the need to take back control. She took a deep breath.

'There must be the equivalent of land registry in Spain. We could find out who the registered owner of the property is.'

'Maybe.'

'It must be possible.' It was obvious that Wendy didn't know what to say and she smiled in what Sara considered to be a 'yes dear, there there' kind of way.

'Shall we go back, then? The phone signal is ridiculously feeble out here and I can't see the screen in the sunlight.' Sara marched back towards the car park, and Wendy scurried after her, carrying their joint possessions, abandoned by Sara in her haste.

Back home in Stratford-upon-Avon, Sara tapped wildly on her laptop. A crow of triumph as she found the right department to search was followed by hissed curse when the Spanish Land Registry showed the property owner to be one Graham Edward Parker.

'I don't fucking believe it.'

Sara didn't care that Wendy looked disapproving. She was evidently amazed to hear the normally calm Sara swear like that, Wendy stayed silent while Sara raged. Finally, she ran out of steam, after yelling about what she would do to Graham Edward Parker when she next laid hands on him, Sara could feel herself getting carried away. At 'scooping him out and using him as a houseboat,' Wendy interrupted, 'It's just his name. Not "Mr and Mrs". Micaela's name isn't mentioned there.'

'And nor is mine. Which cuts me out of the picture as well, though, doesn't it? What the hell's he playing at, telling me he borrowed it? Ah, to hell with him. I'm gonna tear his rotten, cheating, lying head off. I need a fag.'

'You don't smoke.'

'Well I might start right now.'

Wendy burst out laughing.

The British Panacea

Martha was being prepped for surgery. The anaesthetist, cheerful, bespectacled and seeming to Martha far too young to have such a responsible position, tried to persuade her to have a local block.

'No, I'd rather not, thank you.'

'The recovery time'll be much quicker.' His Liverpool accent made all his words smile, and Martha found herself warming to him.

'I'm sure it would be, but my imagination is far too active.'

'Fair enough.' Clearly, he knew when he had met his match. 'Well, I'll see you in theatre in about twenty minutes, then.' He nodded at Jude, who was standing next to Martha, turned in his ridiculous white plastic clogs and strode away, whistling cheerfully.

Martha was nervous. The only other time she'd been in hospital was over half a century ago, when Graham was born, and that had hardly been the joyful occasion it should have been. Even now she could remember the shame and embarrassment when the nurses stressed 'Miss Edwards,' as though her lack of a respectable honorific offended them. The swinging sixties, they called it. Cirencester hadn't swung. It hadn't even wobbled a bit. Martha was viewed as a disgrace to her family; a figure of notoriety and gossip. Her mother had tried to get her to have the baby adopted. 'You needn't even see it,' she'd said. 'It could go to a good family, one that wants a child, that could provide for it. A proper family with two parents, that's what a child needs. You could carry on with your own life in a decent fashion. Have it adopted, Martha, please.'

Martha had been horrified, distraught at her mother's words. 'We're talking about your grandchild, not an "*it*", I thought you loved me! How could you even say such a thing?'

Nobody visited her while she was in the hospital—no loving father, eager to see his new baby—no doting grandparents weighed down with flowers and teddy bears and lovingly hand-knitted white layettes. She and baby Graham had been encouraged to move away to a bedsit in Gloucester, where they survived on weekly cheques from her father, unbeknownst to her mother, and the occasional unwilling hand-out from the baby's father too, until he'd lost interest and gone back to his wife, his mid-life foray into a Bohemian existence over. It was only when Martha had met Bernard Parker that life had become bearable, and he'd taken them both on.

'A ready-made family,' he'd said, when she protested. 'How lucky can one man get?' He'd proposed three times before she finally said yes.

They'd never told Graham. They'd hoped to have more children of their own, but somehow it had just never happened. Graham had always believed himself to be their beloved only son, until Bernard's vindictive sister Barbara had opened her stupid, vicious mouth at his funeral.

'Why are you upset?' she'd snapped at Graham. 'Of course, he wasn't your REAL father. You were just a by-blow. We were never told who sired you. I'm not sure that woman even knew herself.'

Barbara was a spiteful bitch, thought Martha. She'd always had it in for them both, believing that somehow she had cheated her brother of a proper wife and family.

There had been the most enormous row.

'Of course he was your father. He raised you, he loved you, and he cherished you. He was so proud of you. We both were—are. I am still. We are a family, how could he NOT be your father? The rest is just biology.'

Graham had said some very cruel things. He'd stormed out of the wake, and vanished. Martha waited for him to calm down and come home, reasoning that he would understand, once he thought about what she'd said, but he never had. Twenty-seven years of being alone. A single tear rolled down her cheek. All those wasted years.

'Ready, Martha?' Jude caught sight of the tear. 'Hey, no need to be afraid. You'll be back here before you know it.' She smudged the tear away with her thumb and gave Martha a big smile. 'I brought a chair—I thought you'd prefer it to a trolley—it's more dignified.'

Martha pulled herself together, nodded and sat in the wheelchair.

'So, they explained the procedure to you? Have you got any questions?'

'Apparently I'll have full use of my hand again afterwards.'

'Yes. You'll need some physio, I expect.'

'Right. I suppose I'll have to stop giving the piano

recitals though?'

Jude stared at her, surprised and concerned, and then realised she was being teased. Laughing, she turned Martha's chair into the anteroom. 'Here we go. I'll see you when you get back.'

As the nurse walked away, Martha wondered who she reminded her of. She seemed familiar, somehow.

Jude was grabbing a quick coffee and a sandwich on the hop while she filled in the never-ending pile of paperwork at the nurses' station, transferring the same details from one form to the next. She smiled as she added the details of Martha's safe delivery to theatre. Martha Parker, nee Edwards, born May 5th, 1942. She was about the same age as Jude's own mother, but somehow Martha seemed older than Dilys. She had the same forthright attitude to life, though. Perhaps it was a generational thing.

Next of kin: Graham Edward Parker, son. Jude took a big bite of the cheese and celery sandwich that had been the only one left on the shelf when she nipped into the hospital shop. She wasn't wild about celery but at least it gave the flabby sandwich some resistance when she bit into it. Chewing, she kept typing with one hand.

Curious thing, coincidence. Exactly the same name as Keira, Poppy and Robbie's dad. Except this Graham Parker was still most definitely alive. Her lips tightened as she thought about the photograph that someone had sent her only yesterday. Surely Graham wouldn't have done such a brutal thing to her; what kind of man lied to a woman pregnant with his twins, and then faked his own death? Why would he do that to her, or to his own kids? And who the hell was the woman in the picture? Sarah? No, not Sarah, *Sara*. Maybe he wasn't the same man she'd known. Maybe he'd been brain-damaged in the accident, forgotten her, rebuilt a new life without ever knowing about his family?

She was clutching at straws, she knew. That didn't explain the early morning phone call from his friend. She shook her head in disgust as a bell rang, summoning her. She put the remains of her sandwich down with a sigh, swigged a quick mouthful of coffee while it was still reasonably hot, then got to her feet and went to see what Gloria wanted.

It was the strangest dream. Martha was holding hands with Graham, who seemed to be about three years old. She knew she was dreaming, but it was so real. Those little red Clarks sandals with half a daisy cut into the toes, that bright yellow jumper that she'd knitted with such care, the sleeves rolled over a couple of times at the wrists where she'd got the measurements wrong. They were at the swings in the park. She lifted him into the old-fashioned toddler seat with the metal bar across the front, and pulled the swing back. The chains on the swing made her hands smell of rusty iron.

'Higher, Mummy, higher.'

The sky was brilliantly blue and she could hear birdsong and an ice cream van playing "Waltzing Matilda" in the background.

She was pushing and pushing, loving the sound of

his giggles as he sailed through the air. 'Time to go and feed the ducks, my lovely.' It was the only way to get him off the swing, she'd learned. She reached out to lift him out of the toddler seat and was vaguely surprised to watch his skin turn to a warm coffee colour as she hoisted him into the air. It didn't matter, she'd just forgotten, that was all. This was her darling little Graham, so what if he had brown skin now? His eyes, his smile were the same. Just the same. Darling Graham.

'Martha? Hello, Martha? Can you open your eyes for me?'

The voice penetrated the joy of the sunny playground and Graham disappeared again.

'You're back on the ward, Martha. Everything went well. I'm just going to take a few obs, OK?'

'Mmm.'

Her mouth was dry, her eyelids heavy. Vaguely, she became aware of a tightening on her upper arm, and frowned. Her arm was so heavy.

'Good girl. We'll let you sleep for a while. Nearly done.'

She drifted back to sleep. A different dream.

The first time she met Bernard Parker, she hadn't liked him much. He was too needy, too grateful for the smallest attention. His trousers had come down on one heel and he had a frayed cuff on his shirt. He didn't take care of his things properly. He was too thin, and he had a hesitation in his speech that wasn't quite a stammer. He was a lot older than Martha as well, nearly 40 to her 25. But he was kind, and he was funny, and he loved

65

Graham as though he were his own son. Never once did he ask about the boy's father, he just took at face value her blunt statement, 'He's mine. It's just him and me.'

Their dates had always been dates for three. He took them to the zoo; on the bus to the seaside at Weston-super-Mare, where he had steadied a round-eyed Graham on what he assured him was the fastest donkey in the whole wide world. Graham had adored Bernard from the time they first met, and Bernard had reciprocated that love.

In her dream, Martha could see the two of them in a series of moving images, like a montage: holding hands as they jumped waves in the cold sea; laughing together at the Punch and Judy show; wrapped up warm in matching hand-knitted scarves going to the rugby; having a pint at the pub. The images flitted through her sleeping brain in rapid succession. Graham and Bernard playing chess, watching TV, climbing a hill to fly a kite and then, suddenly, shockingly, a coffin. Flowers. Graham, at first sympathetic and loving, holding her hand tightly, and then his angry face, shouting, shouting, shouting.

'Martha? Martha. It's OK, you're just having a dream, it's only a dream. Martha.'

Foggily, she came to, confused. She stared blearily at the woman's face. A nurse?

'Martha, you're in hospital. You had a fall, at home, yes? You've had an operation on your wrist. Remember? The anaesthetics have given you funny dreams. You're quite safe. Everything's OK now.'

The nurse waited calmly for this to filter through, holding Martha's good hand comfortingly all the time she was speaking.

'What's the time?' Martha's voice was slurred with sleep, and she swallowed, trying to drag herself from the distressing dream.

'Half-past five. It's still a couple of hours till breakfast. Do you want a cup of tea?'

The British panacea. 'Yes. Please.'

The nurse patted her hand reassuringly and seemed to reappear magically only seconds later, holding a plastic mug. 'It's hot, be careful. I'll put it here. Do you want help sitting up?'

Normality returned. Martha focused on the nurse.

'You're Karen?'

'I am.'

'Was I such a dragon?'

Karen grinned, turning a bit pink.

'I'm sorry you heard me say that.'

'Was I?'

'You were pretty scary, yes. Surely you knew that?'

'Maybe.' Martha smiled wryly. 'It's the only way to control thirty-six rowdy nine-year-olds, you know— fear.'

Karen laughed.

'My son's seventeen. Got any good tips to keep him in check? I can't scare someone who's a whole head taller than me these days.'

Seventeen. Martha remembered Karen when she had been in her class, a stout little girl with bitten fingernails and always sporting a plaster on her knee from one bump or another. Where had the years gone?

'You could stand on the stairs, maybe?' It was a feeble joke but they both chuckled.

'So, will you be having any visitors today?'

'No, I don't think so.'

'Your husband?'

'He died, dear. He was much older than me. He's been dead more than twenty-five years.'

'I'm sorry.'

'Oh, time passes. You get used to things.'

Karen nodded. 'You do.'

'He was young, though. Sixty-two. It's no age, is it?'

'I guess not, no. Was it his heart?'

'No. Leukaemia. We were on holiday and he just couldn't stay awake. We went to the local doctor there, who sent us straight to a hospital; they did some tests, but ten days later he was dead. It was a terrible shock.'

'That must have been awful.'

'Strange to think that I'm more than ten years older now than he ever got…He'd be nearly ninety.'

There was a short silence. Karen put the cover straight on Martha's bed and looked at the clock. 'I'd better get on. Drink your tea while it's hot.'

'I will. Thank you, Karen.'

'You're welcome, Mrs Parker.'

'Martha.'

'Martha.'

Sara dressed smartly in her favourite work dress, a grey linen shift from Whistles. She'd psyched herself up, all ready for a long day catching up at the office, and she was just making herself a cup of tea when the letterbox rattled and she heard the thud of post landing on the hall floor. Her heart seemed to sink and pound at the same time, if that was possible. She decided wilfully to ignore it for as long as she could, shoving two slices of bread in the toaster and looking in the back of the cupboard for the Marmite instead. Defiantly staring out into the garden, with her back to the hallway, she grabbed the toast as soon as it popped up, juggling it a little to save her fingers, put her breakfast on a tray, and took it over to the window-seat, being careful not to glance down the hall towards the front door as she did so.

The toast tasted of cardboard in her dry mouth.

Fuming, she stomped down the hall, telling herself that this was ridiculous, that it would be the usual rubbish, a flyer from Domino's Pizza, a magazine from a holiday company and an invitation to buy a remarkable armchair that would tilt you, lift you up, and as far as the makers were concerned, probably be able to tell you your horoscope for the day as well. Nobody else worried about their post before they even saw it, she was getting paranoid. She stared down at the post scattered on the wood block floor. See, harmless. If you didn't count the credit card bill that jostled for space with the rest, she'd even been quite accurate. Then she saw the plain brown stiffened envelope, addressed by hand. She recognised the writing, and the hairs stood up on her arms. Sara HAD to go to work today. She hadn't got time for this stupid game. This was just malice, that's all. Just someone trying to cause trouble. Taking Wendy's advice, she put the envelope straight into the flip-top bin in the kitchen without opening it, dropped a soggy teabag on it for good measure, and went upstairs to put on her make-up. If her eyeliner wobbled, it wasn't because her hands were shaking.

Micaela Fernandez Parker stood smiling brightly at the weary passengers as they finally disembarked. 'Goodbye. Thank you. Have a good day.' The passenger line seemed endless. 'Goodbye.' Her feet were killing her and she wanted a long, hot soak in the bath, with plenty of bubbles and maybe a large gin for good measure. These back-to-back flights were a killer, but at least she had a few days off now. Inwardly, Micaela's brain was whirling, but she made like the swan she was always encouraging her crew to imagine, and kept smiling. 'Thank you.' Outwardly calm, efficient, super-helpful and friendly, Micaela never seemed to be ruffled by anything.

As the last passenger hit the steps, her team did the final cabin checks before quitting the A380 with relief, immaculate and poised to the last. Forget the tube. She summoned an Uber, and was heading home to her flat within fifteen minutes, changing with relief out of the regulation heels she'd been wearing for more hours than she cared to think about. Her feet sent a message of thanks as she laced up her trainers in the back of the cab.

The front door to her flat was heavy to push over the pile of post that had accumulated since she went away. At least the postie had read the note on her letterbox and shoved everything right through this time.

Nothing said "empty flat" quite as loudly as three-day-old mail sticking out of a door. The free newspapers were the worst culprits. Whoever read those things anyway? She bet most of the freesheets went straight from the doormat into the recycling without even a glance at the headline. Stooping, she grabbed the pile and then shuffled the envelopes like playing cards as she made her way to the kitchen. Far too much junk, a couple of bills, and—ah—this was the one she'd been waiting for. She recognised the Private Investigator's writing on the plain brown envelope. Eagerly, she ripped it open, keen to read the progress of her campaign. Inside was a letter and some numbered photocopies of photographs.

Dear Ms Fernandez,

This is to update you of the project up until the end of last week—

The first swathe of photographs were delivered week beginning 12th, as discussed. As yet, no great reaction has been noted.

—SP drove to Oxford to visit the Pitt Rivers Museum with a female friend, shortly after receiving her copy of photo (1), attached. This appears to be lucky chance. She certainly didn't stay long.

—JP continues working at the Gloucester Royal Infirmary. The children are now all school-aged, and out-of-school care is shared between JP and her mother. JP is, in fact, using her natural surname, Richards. I can find no evidence of a marriage taking place. She received photo (2). As far as I could tell, she has not reacted in any way.

—MP has recently been hospitalised, following a domestic accident. By fortunate coincidence, she has been admitted to the Gloucester Royal where JP(R) is working as a nurse. As far as I am aware, no connections have occurred between MP and JP(R). MP received photo (3), as attached.

I have this morning sent out the second wave of contact, as planned, and await further instruction.

Yours faithfully, etc., etc.

Micaela felt a slight tinge of guilt when she read about the old woman's accident. She hoped the 'domestic' nature wasn't to do with shock. Ah well, there was nothing she could do about it now. By now they'd all been alerted to the fact that their 'perfect' Graham had feet of clay, if they didn't already know that. Fairly soon they'd realise how much of a failure he'd made of his life. The wheels were beginning to turn a little faster already, the next delivery should whet their curiosity a little more. Then, when they were really unsettled, she'd send out her invitations. She had to make them really keen to find out what was happening then maybe she could get some help in sorting him out. This wasn't anything she could do alone.

By lunchtime, Sara found she couldn't concentrate at all. It was as though the package in the kitchen bin was sending out a beat, like a war drum. What was that film called? Jumanji. It was just like that. Shaking her head at her own foolishness, she invented a document she'd left at home, and grateful for the fact it was only a ten-minute drive back to her house, got in her car.

Furious with herself, she left the car on the road rather than turning into her drive and scurried down the side of the house, hoping that this way Wendy wouldn't notice her arrival. That was the problem with living in a semi-detached property, even in a nice part of town like this. Your 'other half' had a pretty good idea of every move you made.

Her hand shook as she fumbled with the back door key, and flipping open the bin lid with distaste, she grabbed the now slightly soggy envelope, shoving it angrily into her vast canvas shoulder bag. She grabbed a couple of random documents from the desk in her study for verisimilitude and shot back to the office.

Martha's wrist ached horribly under the blue padded cuff. It was visiting time, and her neighbour Gloria's entire extended family seemed to have turned up, completely disregarding the notice that asked for "three visitors only per bed, please", as though the furniture was being visited rather than its occupant. They brought with them vast armfuls of glossy magazines and carrier bags full of food, a teddy bear with enormous eyes and a soulful expression, and three huge, bobbing, gas-filled foil balloons, each exhorting Gloria to Get Well Soon. They sat on the bed, perched on the windowsill, and filled the armchair like a flock of brightly coloured jackdaws, cackling with laughter and interrupting each other at full volume.

'Can we nick your chair, love? We'll give it back if you get a visitor, promise.'

Martha nodded and closed her eyes, turning her face away.

'She's not very friendly, is she, Mum?' hissed one of the women, in what for her was clearly only a whisper. 'Bet she's a barrel of laughs.'

'She's all right. She only had her op late yesterday afternoon. I think she's quite drugged-up still.'

'Oh. What's she in for then? Women's trouble?'

Martha could feel the fury rising. She resisted the temptation to wave her enormously padded arm and sling at them.

'No. Bust her arm, bashed her head and tipped the kettle over herself.'

'Oh, nasty. Poor old thing.'

There was a silence while Gloria's visitors stared at Martha in mute sympathy.

'Shall I tie one of your balloons on the end of her bed, Grannie Glo? It might cheer her up a bit.'

'You do that, my love. That's kind of you. Leave her one of them bags of sweets on her table, too. I don't think she's got any family. She's not had any visitors, and she came in all by herself.'

'Oh, the poor love.'

There was a general chorus of sympathy from the massed relatives. Even with her eyes shut, she could feel their collected gaze on her. She willed herself not to blush under their scrutiny. Martha didn't know whether

74

to keep pretending to be asleep or miraculously wake up and be drawn into the conversation. Unable to face the latter, she kept her eyes closed. The chat levels rose again, and despite the noise she dozed off, only to be woken seemingly just moments later by the bell declaring that visiting time was over.

Gloria's family had started to gather their things noisily, and much hugging and kissing goodbye was going on. A small girl of about six or seven was standing between Gloria and Martha's beds. Seeing Martha open her eyes, she beamed at her.

'Hello, I'm Tiffany-Marie. That balloon's for you. What's your name? Does your arm hurt? Will you be here for days and days? You've got a black eye. Did someone thump you? I had a black eye once 'cos I fell off the slide. That balloon's for you. I tied it on all by myself. I can do double knots now.'

'Tiff, leave the lady alone. She's poorly.'

Martha smiled at the child.

'Thank you for the balloon. It's lovely. That was very kind of you.' She smiled at the woman she presumed to be Tiffany-Marie's mother. 'Thank you.'

'No problem, love. Auntie Glo's running out of room, spread the love, you know. D'you need anything, love? You just missed the tea wagon, shall I run and get you a cuppa tea? No trouble. Tiff, find the tea lady. Tell her the lady next to Grannie Glo's woken up. Fetch her a cup of tea. Sugar, love?'

Her attention was back to Martha.

'No, no, thank you—'

'No sugar, but get her a few biscuits Tiff, there's a

good girl.'

The child darted off.

'Will she manage, carrying hot tea?'

'That one? She could MAKE you a better cup of tea than the gnat's piss they serve here, never mind just carrying it.'

Tiffany-Marie returned, triumphant, with a plastic mug of tea in one rather sticky hand and a clutch of rich tea biscuits in the other.

'There you go. The good biscuits was all gone, there was just these. Sorry. I got you plenty though. They're dunkers.'

She put the mug down carefully and stacked the biscuits in a neat pile next to the steaming drink. 'See you tomorrow. You didn't tell me what your name was.'

Surprised, Martha said 'My name's Martha Parker.'

'See you tomorrow, Auntie Martha.' There was general laughter from the family, waiting by the door.

Martha found herself waving at the cheerful child as she bounced out, chatting loudly and waving at anyone who looked in her direction.

'She's a tonic, our Tiff, isn't she? You can't never feel down for long if she's around.'

Martha had to agree.

Second Letters Arrive

Back at the familiar safety of her desk, Sara retrieved the latest envelope from her bag, and held it in both hands, considering what to do. She stared at it dispassionately: the teabag hadn't done it any favours, one corner was soggy and fragile. Wavering, she put it down again and went to get herself a coffee.

'Penny for them?'

'Sorry?'

Matt, junior partner, smiled easily. 'You were miles away there.'

'You don't know how right you are, Matt. I was in Spain.'

'Oh, I'm so jealous. Just look at it out there now. Where the hell did that come from?' Matt had to raise his voice over the noise of the rain hitting the window, as a sudden summer storm hit with a vengeance. He smiled at her, nodding his head at the streaky glass. 'What I wouldn't give to be on a beach in Spain right now.'

Sara smiled politely, raising her mug in a 'cheers' motion and turned away. Closing the door to her little office, she moved swiftly across the room, and plonked the coffee down on the desk with a thud, where it sent little wavelets over the top of the cup, splashing the polished wood. Annoyed even further, she blotted the desk with a couple of tissues before a watermark set, then she snatched up the offending envelope and ripped it open viciously, sending the pages spinning out.

The first sheet had two words on it:

EN VENTA

She stared at it blankly for a second before comprehension and recognition dawned. This was the house they usually holidayed in, the house that Graham owned, she thought bitterly. Up for sale. An English translation had been stapled to the Spanish details, presumably for her benefit.

> FOR SALE BY AUCTION, CONTENTS 23 JULY 2017, VILLA 24TH JULY 2017
> Fully-furnished, three beds three baths, detached, gated community, well situated, sea views. More details available on request.

What? The house AND its contents? Was that usual in Spain? She couldn't work out what was going on. Turning the tea-stained papers over sheet-by-sheet gave no further clues. Shaking the envelope produced another of the small, bright pink post-it notes, this time with the message. " I thought you'd be interested to read this, Sara. I wonder whether you know what he needs all that money for?"

Chilled, Sara sat down in the leather chair, feeling sick. This was a vendetta. There was a tap on the door, and Matt stuck his cheery face into the room. 'Sara, could you just cast an—are you OK?' Solicitously, he came in, and closed the door quietly behind him. 'Are you feeling OK? You've gone really white. Can I get you a glass of water or something?'

'I'm fine.' She waved him away, dismissing her nausea. 'Something I ate, I think. Maybe I shouldn't have come in after all. Not to worry. What did you want, Matt?'

'Oh, it doesn't matter—it was only a second opinion on something—I'll get Chris to read it.'

'No, no, I'm fine, really. Pass it over.'

Unwillingly, he handed her the sheaf of paper.

'So, what am I looking for?'

'The usual. Loopholes, typos—as SurAlan says—a fresh pair of eyes.'

He smiled, seeing if she'd pick up the reference. 'The Apprentice' was a keen subject for derision in the office every year. They generally ran a sweepstake on who would be fired each week, and they argued fiercely in the run-up to the final episode, the office splitting into two distinct, competitive camps. Apart from last year, Sara thought, distractedly. That chap had been a shoo-in from the start. She nodded at Matt, struggling to present her ordinary, professional self. Concentrate, Sara, concentrate.

'Fine. Give me ten minutes. I'll drop it back to you.'

There was no hint of humour in her brittle smile. Sensing his dismissal, he left, though not without casting a concerned glance back at her as he opened the door. She pretended not to notice, turning the pages as if she was already enthralled by the document, and reaching for her cooling coffee with the other hand. Autopilot took her through the pages, circling a stray apostrophe and striking out a repeated word without taking in what the words actually meant when strung together.

He would wait for a few more minutes, she was sure. On Google, she found the Spanish estate agency pages and brought up the details for 'Casa Nuevo', selecting the little red, white and blue flag that gave her the English language option. Here, she found a slightly more fulsome description.

For Sale: Nice house close to the sea.
Villa near to the beach, distributed in three bedrooms, three bathrooms, swimming pool, summer kitchen, open panoramic views, O.I.R.O. 500000E.

Half a million Euros? Where had he got the sort of money to buy that without a word? She attached the details to an email and sent it to Wendy, with one line:

'Do you fancy a trip to Calpe next week? I'll pay.'

She spent the rest of the day clearing her backlog of work and writing clear instructions for her colleagues to follow. Walking into the main office with an armful of documents, she called for a moment's attention.

'Sorry. Sorry to interrupt, folks. Something personal has come up, and I'm going to be out of the office intermittently for the next week or so while I sort things out. These are all of my on-going projects. I've attached notes. Can I share them out amongst you? They only need nursemaiding. The main work is complete.'

She passed the work around. Concerned faces asked if she was all right, whether they could do anything to help? She knew they would be speculating on the nature of the 'personal something' the moment she was gone. Illness, death, divorce? The usual list. I bet none of them think of an absentee bigamist husband with a secret home, about to come into half a million euros without a word to his wife of twenty-six years, she thought acidly. Fobbing off their questions politely but in a manner that didn't encourage any curious enquiries, she went back into her office, closed her computer down, picked up the Spanish documents and her laptop, her bag, jacket, umbrella and keys, and made for the door.

'Do you need any help?' It was Matt again, catching her jacket as it slipped from her grasp. 'Let me walk you to your car.'

Silently nodding her thanks, she passed him the laptop and they left the office. The rain had stopped and the sun was shining again. The car park glistened with steaming puddles.

'Are you sure that you're OK, Sara? Can I help in any way?'

'Thanks, Matt, but I'm absolutely fine.'

'Shall I call you later to check?' His dark eyes were full of concern.

'No, no, really, I'll be OK.' She looked at him and gave him a smile that only involved her mouth. 'Thanks though. I appreciate the thought.'

He nodded, putting her stuff onto the back seat of the BMW.

'But if you change your mind?'

'Yes. Thanks.'

He surprised them both, bending into the car and

kissing her cheek. There was an awkward silence.

'Sorry.' He seemed confused. 'Look after yourself.'

'Right.'

Putting the car into reverse she backed out of the car park waving in the general direction of his legs as she passed him. What had just happened there? Dismissing the kiss as a minor complication that she didn't need, she drove home rather faster than she should have done, scattering the gravel on her drive yet again as she turned the car sharply in to the space in front of the living room window. Mentally, she made a resolution to get the area tarmacked.

Wendy was waiting keenly at her own bedroom window, and seeing the car, waved boisterously. Sara beckoned her to come in and left the front door open. Through the party wall, she heard Wendy hammering down the stairs. She moved the papers from the settee onto the glass-topped coffee table, and sank down gratefully into the squashy cream leather, indicating that Wendy should do the same.

'He's selling that house then?'

'So it would seem.'

'Half a million Euros, though, Sara. That's a hell of a lot of money for a second home. Well, it sounds it, anyway. How much is that in real money?'

Sara didn't bother working it out. 'It's an auction. It might not make that much.'

'Do you want to go to Spain for the auction? Is that what you meant?'

'Yes. Yes, exactly that. He might be there. Then I can pin the bastard down with the evidence.'

'But what if he's not there though?'

There was a pause. Sara hadn't even entertained that as an option.

'He will be. I just know him. He'll want to stand unobtrusively in the background and watch the bidding, and to check the auctioneer isn't diddling him at the same time. He'll be rubbing his hands together already, at the prospect of all that cash.'

'Where is he at the moment?'

'USA, somewhere, I think.'

'When did you last hear from him?'

'Just a couple of days ago. He texted to say he wasn't able to phone, lots of business meetings and unreliable signal, probably.'

'I thought you two spoke every day?'

'We used to but for the last eighteen months we've got out of the habit. We text, mostly. Isn't that what everyone does now? Especially when there isn't much to say.'

'Sara, aren't you worried?'

Sara looked at her friend. 'Between you and me?'

'Yes?'

Sara looked down at her hands as the silence ticked on. The grandfather clock in the hall struck six. Eventually, she shook her head. 'I'm fucking terrified.'

The Treasure

It was visiting time again. Martha was amazed to see Janet arrive at her bedside, almost unrecognisable and so smart in a flowery summer dress and matching soft blue jacket. She was clutching a bunch of grapes, a large bag and a copy of Bella. 'Thought you might like some company, Mrs P. How are you feeling?'

'How did you know where I was?'

'Mrs Knight next door told me when I couldn't get an answer this morning. I went next door in case she had a key. I was worried about you.'

Martha was overwhelmed.

'I brought tissues.' Janet plonked her bag on her knee and produced a seemingly endless stream of goodies, in the manner of an elderly Mary Poppins and naming each item as she did so, almost as though she wasn't sure that Martha would recognise them, away from their proper places in her house. 'Squash—because the water always tastes odd in hospitals. Tissues—because you've had a shock. Rescue remedy—to perk you up. The paperback that was by your bed? I put a piece of paper in to keep your page. A clean nightie. Hand cream. Grapes, of course. You aren't allowed to visit hospitals without bringing grapes, are you? A magazine in case you can't face reading a whole book.'

Martha opened the tissues, and taking one, wiped the tears flowing down her cheeks. 'Janet, that's so kind of you. You've thought of everything.'

'Rubbish. You'd do the same for me. I know you would.' Janet smiled dismissively at an openly curious Gloria. 'Afternoon, you all right?' Ignoring any answer, Janet busied herself putting the things away in the tall locker next to Martha's bed. 'Have you got any washing?' She found the plastic bag on the bottom shelf of the locker and tucked into her shopping bag.

'Oh no, you don't need to do that.'

Janet nodded at the plaster on Martha's arm.

'You can hardly do it yourself, can you? It won't take me five minutes to rinse a few smalls, don't you worry. So, when are they letting you out?' Her tone was brisk.

'I don't know, they won't say for certain. By the end of the week, maybe?'

'Typical. They'd chuck you out all on your own at the weekend when there's nobody available to check on you. You want to stay in here till Monday. Get everything set up at home first. How long will you be in plaster, do you know?'

'Six weeks, apparently.'

Janet breathed in, meaningfully. 'And how are you expected to cope, living all alone? How will you get a bath? You won't be able to drive or carry shopping, even squeezing toothpaste onto your toothbrush is going to be a challenge. Oh, I'm sorry, I didn't mean to make you cry again, I didn't think.'

Martha was furious with herself. She pulled more tissues from the box angrily.

'You've had a shock, Mrs P., that's all. It'll do you good, shedding a few tears.'

Embarrassed, Martha took a moment to breathe

deeply and pull herself together.

'Oh, I almost forgot, I brought your post. I'll put it in your drawer, shall I, until you feel up to it? I'm sure it's nothing that won't wait. I threw out the obvious junk, you don't want that cluttering up the place.'

Janet stayed for half an hour, chatting about inconsequential things. The cat next door that was threatening the fish in their shrinking pond, the remarkable change in the weather, how she had borrowed Doreen Knight's key, remembered to water all Martha's indoor plants and had a word with the milkman. 'So, you don't need to worry about anything at home. I've got it all in hand. Would you like me to talk with the nurses? I'll tell them that you can't go home at the weekend. I'm used to it. When my Robert was ill, I got used to dealing with The System.'

Martha could hear the capital letters in Janet's voice. Robert had been Janet's husband, who had died a few years previously.

'I will. I'll do that for you right now, Mrs P, you're not up to being home alone just yet. Have they contacted your son?'

'No. No, I don't want them to worry him.' As Martha said it, she knew somehow that Janet was thinking; 'And you don't know where he is', but noted that Janet shrewdly said nothing, merely patted Martha's good hand in a friendly way.

'Right then, I'll be off. The bus goes at twenty past, and I don't want to miss that. I'll come again tomorrow, shall I?'

'You don't have to.'

'I know. But I'd like to. And it does you good, seeing a familiar face, doesn't it.' Bending, she kissed Martha on the cheek. 'Be good.'

Martha, surprised, smiled at her, swallowing down the wretched tears that threatened again. 'I will. Thank you, Janet. Thank you, for everything.'

She saw Janet walk briskly towards an unsuspecting nurse, determination in her stride. 'Good afternoon. Could I have a word about Mrs Parker please?'

'That your friend?' asked Gloria, visitor-less for once.

Martha was about to say, 'No, she's my cleaning lady,' when the truth hit her. 'Yes, that's right. I don't know what I'd do without her.' She reached across to her locker. 'Would you like a grape?'

Viable Arguments

Wendy was online, checking how swiftly she could update her passport. 'Short of driving to the passport office, and sitting there while they print the bloody thing, it looks like there's no chance I'll get it done in time,' she said. 'I'm so angry with myself for not noticing it'd run out. It's not like me to be so careless, but we weren't going abroad this year, what with having the new kitchen and everything, so I guess I just let it slip. I'm really sorry, Sara.'

'It doesn't matter. It was a ridiculous, impetuous idea. I have no idea what I thought we could do…I can hardly barge in there and demand they stop the sale or they give me half the proceeds or something can I? Like you say, he might not even be there.'

'I still feel bad that I can't help you.'

'No, really, don't. I'm sure I read somewhere that they don't encourage vendors to go to auctions. They're too intense, too invested, you know? They drive the punters away, apparently.'

'You could always go on your own, Sara. You've been to Spain lots of times. You'd know what to do.'

'Mm.'

'Or you could take someone else, maybe?'

'No. I'm not telling anyone else about this mess. Not any of it. Please don't you tell anyone either.'

Guiltily, Wendy thought about the discussions that she and her husband had been having since first the wedding picture had landed on Sara's doormat. 'I, um, I may have mentioned it to Brian.' She shifted uneasily from one foot to the other, awkward in her admission.

Sara shot her a severe look.

'He won't say anything. Really. He won't, Sara.'

'It's too late now if he has, I guess.'

'He won't. I'll get him to come round and swear to you if you like.'

'No, there's no need for that. Not if you say he won't.'

Crossing her fingers out of sight, Wendy reassured Sara.

'I'm absolutely positive he won't mention a word to anyone.' Hopefully he wouldn't laugh about it with his mates down the pub after his usual five-a-side match tonight. He'd never got on with Graham, saw him as stuck up and snooty. Brian would relish Graham's downfall. With luck though, his team would win tonight and they'd all be laughing about the football. Wendy's smile was just a little frozen as she left Sara's kitchen.

Jude was pleased that she was coming to the end of her shift pattern at last and she was looking forward to a few days off. She could do with a break, and she knew her mum would be glad to have some space without being tied to the kids and their school times. She would never have managed to hold down her job without Dilys's help. She decided to buy her some flowers on the way home as thanks, something bright and cheerful. Dilys loved splashy flowers. Jude preferred the sort that you could smell before you saw them, lilies, freesias, that kind of thing. She wondered if it was too early in the year to find her mother a bunch of sunflowers. Morrisons might have some. She looked at the clock. Two more hours to go. She started on the meds round. 'Mrs Parker.'

'Martha.'

'Martha.' Jude smiled. 'How's your pain?'

Dispensing mild painkillers, and promising stronger drugs if those didn't work, Jude checked Martha's bracelet before handing her the paper cup with two white capsules in it.

'You had a visitor, then.'

'Yes. Janet. She's my treasure.'

Unusual phrase, thought Jude.

'That's nice. She had a word with Sister. I gather you're staying till Monday.'

'I am?'

'You are. She fought a good case for you. I hope you've got a good book, mind you. Weekends are really boring in hospital.'

'I'll be fine.'

'You will.'

Jude smiled and went to move on. 'I'm off for a few days now, so if I don't see you again I hope you have a speedy recovery.'

'Thank you. Thanks for your care, dear.'

'You're very welcome.'

That was the strange thing about this job, Jude mused. You got to know one aspect of folk. Sometimes the best, sometimes the worst, and then with luck you never saw them again. Sometimes, people she didn't recognise at all stopped her in the street. People in their ordinary, everyday clothes, wearing make-up, and with immaculate hair, smiling people who recognised her easily as the kind nurse, whereas she had trouble relating them to the pale, worried, ill people she had known. Clothes and circumstance, she supposed, made all the difference.

The hands on the clock moved annoyingly slowly. She needed this break. Robbie was getting to be quite rebellious when he went to Dilys. She was going to have to restore some ground rules over the next few days, she could tell. Jude was going to take the kids to the seaside on Sunday if the weather held out. Ruth was organising a coach trip for the local Mums Alive group to Weston-super-Mare, or Brean, perhaps, if the tide was out. It wasn't exactly St Tropez, but it would be a laugh, and it would do the kids good to run wild for a bit.

Sara sat in front of her computer. Her mind kept turning in circles and coming back to the same point without a sensible solution, that was the trouble, she thought. Round and round. What was the best thing to do? Half of her wasn't confident enough to go to Spain on her own. The other half, brimming with curiosity and fury in equal measures, was desperate to see what was happening there. Graham hadn't contacted her for nearly a week, the longest time ever in their twenty-six years of marriage.

She had texted a couple of times, trying to be relaxed and non-committal. 'Hello stranger' and 'Are you OK?' But no response had been sent back. She was starting to worry. Tension spread down her neck and across her shoulders and she made a conscious effort to drop them, to relax. She concentrated on her breathing and tried to focus. She really ought to go back to those yoga classes, she thought.

She tried ringing his mobile number, and got the familiar foreign dialling tone that always confused her. Perhaps Graham had forgotten to switch his phone on to roaming, or maybe he'd had it stolen or it had broken. He'd dropped it before once, and there had been a couple of times when he'd misplaced the thing—or so he had said—although now she wondered if he'd told her the truth. Sara knew she was clutching at straws. She didn't want to contemplate the idea that he was ignoring her, that he had left her, that he had made a decision at last and committed himself to the elusive Micaela who he had 'married' in Oxford more than 20 years ago.

The hell with it. Sara brought up the budget airline site and bought a three-day return flight to Alicante, on the grounds that it was easier to regret something you did than wonder forever whether you ought to have done it. At least it would cancel out a few of the 'what if's'. She tried to use the joint credit card, but the system refused it. That was odd. She tried it again, but exactly the same thing happened, the transaction got to a certain point and then the card was rejected. Frustrated, she used her own debit card and saw that this time the transaction had gone through smoothly enough. Relief flooded through Sara as she had a light-bulb moment. That's what had happened, Graham must've had his carry-on bag stolen. His phone, his wallet, his laptop? He must have cancelled the cards so they couldn't be used, and couldn't contact her until he'd had new cards FedExed to his hotel, so he could replace the phone and the laptop. He would be able to explain everything when they met up in Calpe, as they surely would.

Having come up with a viable argument, Sara felt some relief. That would be it. She would hear from him soon that was certain.

Jude

The kids were arguing so loudly when Jude got to her mother's house, that she could hear them even before she let herself in. Dilys was busy in the kitchen, obliviously chopping onions. The row from the sitting room was deafening. Dilys jumped a mile when Jude walked in.

'Bloody hell, Mum, have they been like that long?'

'All day. Don't swear, Jude.' Dilys was talking louder than usual.

'Sorry, Mum. How do you cope?' There was no reply. Dilys continued chopping placidly. 'Mum.'

She looked up, surprised. 'Sorry, Jude. Hang on a sec.'

She took out earphones, and Jude just caught the tinny sound of Radio Two blaring through the little buds.

'Can't hear a thing over that. God, your kids are noisy, aren't they?' She raised her voice. 'Who wants to come in the kitchen and play with the sharp knives?'

'Mum.'

'Oh, it'll be fine. You worry too much.'

She regimented the kids into washing their hands and putting on tea towels as aprons.

'You, Poppy, you can chop the carrots. Use the square board, count your fingers before you start, and only cut the carrots, OK? Be very careful, because this knife is sharp. I'm trusting you to be sensible. Robbie, I need you to cut these mushrooms down the middle like

94

this, OK?'

Robbie was given a butter knife to use.

'Keira. This is difficult. I don't know if you can do this. You might be too little?'

Keira protested that she was as big as Robbie.

'OK. But I'm worried you might hurt yourself if you aren't careful.'

Keira swore she would be very, Very, VERY careful. From a drawer, Dilys took an ancient cheese grater.

'Right. Watch me. You put the cheese in here in little pieces, then you squash it down with the top, and turn this handle. Your hands might be too little to hold it, though. You try.'

Keira tried and failed. Her lip stuck out.

'Hah. No problem. Actually, I've just remembered an even more important job that needs doing.'

Dilys produced a tub of spread and a sliced loaf.

'I need you to butter these six pieces of bread for me so we can make a pudding. Right to the very edges. That's it.'

Tongue jutting out in concentration, Keira set to work.

'That's them sorted, then. Cup of tea, Jude?'

'Mum. The kids are too little for knives.'

'Jude, I brought six kids of my own up successfully without any of you being maimed or beheaded. Your kids are fine. Stop fussing. I'm watchin' them. Go and sit down, you look exhausted. We're OK, aren't we kids?'

There was a chorus of reassurance.

'I've finished now.' This from Robbie, always eager

to be the first to achieve anything. Jude wondered idly whether it was because he was a twin.

'Right.' Dilys turned back to her grandson. 'What do you know about weighing things? See this mark here, by the eight?' Robbie nodded, his face intent as he listened to his Grannie Dil.

Smiling, Jude took the mug gratefully and wandered into the living room, tidying the surface devastation that the kids had left behind them. When Dilys popped her head round the door five minutes later, Jude was fast asleep. She shut the door quietly and turned to the children, a finger to her lips.

'Now then.' She stirred the vegetables into the chicken on the stovetop and put the bread-and-butter pudding into the oven.

'We've got 20 minutes. Let's go and post this birthday card to your Auntie Christine, shall we? Did you all put your kisses on the envelope? Let's go.'

She herded the kids quietly out of the back door.

Graham pounded on the rough plank door. He shifted his weight and the chafing from his sore ankle reminded him that he was a prisoner. He was so bloody thirsty. Where the hell was Micaela?

When Jude finally got home from her mother's house it had gone 8pm. She hustled the kids through the nightly battle of bath and bed, before sitting down in her battered armchair in front of the TV with a sigh. This was when she most felt the loneliness of bringing the kids up alone. This was the time when other people snuggled up with their partners, talked about the funny things that had happened to them during the day, the stresses of work, the ideas that they had for the coming weekend. Against her better nature, she took the photograph out of her bag again and looked at it closely. It definitely was Graham, there were no two ways about it. He looked older, obviously, and he had put on a bit of weight. She tried to work out how old he would be now. He had been 45 when Poppy was born. He had laughed about being a geriatric father.

'I'll be pushing seventy before she even leaves University.'

Jude had laughed with him, promising to keep him young. The age gap between them had never bothered her. Jude was twenty-two when Poppy was born and twenty-four when she was widowed. Although they had never officially been married, she always felt that she might as well have been. The man she had loved, the father of her children, had died and left her alone. What was that if not widowhood? And now this picture had arrived. Who the hell was Sara? Where was Graham? Why had someone sent this to her? Who would do that?

The door opened and a tousled Keira came in, rumpled with sleep.

'I had a bad dream, Mummy.'

Jude opened her arms.

Visits

Alicante airport was quieter than it had been in her previous visits, and Sara was grateful. Packing lightly, she had only brought carry-on luggage with her, so instead of hanging around the luggage carousel with all the other frustrated tourists, she walked straight through customs and smiled at the taxi driver at the front of the rank.

'Calpe, por favor.'

She put on her dark glasses against the brightness of the midday sun and gazed out of the window as the car sped towards Casa Nueva. It was going to be screamingly hot for the next few days, she could tell. The sky had that deep brilliance that promised endless sunshine.

The Airbnb she had found on the net was more than OK; stylish, bright and sunny, with that fabulous, and so familiar, view. By chance it was just a little further up the same road that they always stayed on. In fact, if she stood on tiptoes in one of the bedrooms she could probably see the roof of Casa Nuevo. Sara resisted the urge. She was staying in a flat on the top floor of a similarly designed house, with the owner, Ana, living on the two floors below. Ana was tanned and brisk, addressing Sara in faultless English as she explained the complexities of the hot water system.

'Are you on a touring holiday?'

'No. I'm just here for a few days. I'm quite interested in the house that's up for auction down the road.'

Ana raised an eyebrow. 'The present owner is English, too. He is bankrupt apparently. That house will sell for less than it's worth. He'll take anything, I would think. Everyone knows that. Are you going to make an offer?'

'No. Maybe. I don't know really. I thought I'd go and have a look around it in any case.'

'Do you speak Spanish?'

'Not much. I'm sure they'll understand me, though.'

'Oh yes. You might get a better price if you bid in Spanish though.'

'I'm not really sure I'm buying. I'd just like to look. I used to know the owner.' That was true, she thought. She used to think she knew Graham well, now she wasn't so sure.

'Did you?' Ana looked at her curiously. 'I'd keep that information quiet if I were you. He's not very popular around here. Rumour has it he owes rather a lot of money to too many people. More importantly he owes money to the wrong kind of people, if you know what I'm trying to say?'

Sara was horrified, but managed to keep her expression calm.

'I didn't know him that well,' she said. 'He was more of an acquaintance really.'

Ana raised one beautiful eyebrow again and turned to the door.

'Well, let me know if I can help you with anything. You're very welcome to use our garden and the pool, just go through the glass door at the back of the stairs.'

Sara poured herself a glass from the bottle of white

wine that Ana had left in the fridge for her as a gift and headed out onto the balcony, staring blankly at the endless blue of the sea and sky. Wishing Wendy had been able to come, she made a silent toast. 'Absent friends.'

This cup of tea was much better than yesterday's offering. It depended which of the tea-ladies was on, Martha realised. They were all nice though. Staying in hospital had almost been a rest, if you didn't count the ridiculously early mealtimes, and the horrible plastic cups. Somehow, relinquishing all the day-to-day decisions to the system was calming, reassuring. She was even beginning to get used to Gloria and her incessant chatter. In a strange way, it was almost comforting. Janet had been as good as her word and had visited every day, never stopping very long. 'So I don't wear you out,' but always keeping her up-to-date with the news from home and the reassurance that everything there was fine.

'Have they sorted out some homecare for you yet?'

'I don't think so.'

'I'll go and have a word.'

Martha suspected that the nurses quickly found other things to do each time Janet got to her feet and headed for the nurses station with a determined air. Today she returned triumphantly.

'You're definitely being released on Monday.'

'You make it sound like I'm in prison when you say it like that.'

'You know what I mean. They can offer you two

visits per day to help you with dressing and washing. I said I'd pop in and make you a meal.'

'You don't need to do that.'

'It's no trouble. You'll be worn out when you get home.'

'I'm sure I can manage, Janet.'

'I'm sure you can, but let's see shall we?'

Martha was aware of a change in their relationship. No longer employer and employee, they had moved much closer towards a real friendship.

As Janet left, Gloria's extended family arrived. Tiffany-Marie had grazed knees and a bump on her forehead the size of an egg.

'What ever happened to you?'

Tiff grinned. 'I've got a new bike.'

'Aha. Two wheels?'

'Yes. How did you know?'

'I guessed. Got the hang of it yet?'

'Nearly.'

'Well done you.'

Martha smiled across at Gloria, amused. Tiffany, pleased to be the centre of attention, beamed.

'I didn't cry much when I fell off either.'

Micaela was on the phone to Miguel.

'Is everything set up OK for the auction?'

He grunted. She switched to Spanish. He was more forthcoming.

'Senor Garcia doesn't like to be kept waiting for his money. He is most unhappy.'

'He must have patience. He knows the auction is

happening. Tell him I'm working on it. Have you found Graham Parker yet?'

'No. But we will find him. Are you certain you know nothing?'

'Nothing. I'll let you know if I hear anything at all.'

'Make sure you do.'

Graham thumped on the door with both fists.

'Hello? Can you hear me? Is anybody there? For God's sake, what's the bloody word? Socorro?'

There was no response. He read the note again.

'If they find you, you're a dead man. There's enough food and water here for five days, if you're careful. Use the can in the corner. Stay quiet. They are hunting everywhere for you. The auction is arranged. I'll be back before then. Stay quiet. M.'

He was so hungry, the food was barely enough to keep a mouse alive. He had carefully split it into five parcels on the first day, but each day's portion was eaten by noon, and he was rapidly running out of water, too. It was so hot in this bloody cellar. His phone had died days ago. God knows why he'd wasted the battery sending those texts to Sara. America, for Chrissakes. She thought he was in America. Why the hell had he said that? Stupid. There was no way of charging the phone down here. Graham sat on the earthen floor with a sigh, resigned to his memories. He thought about Jude instead.

She had been irresistible. He'd met her in a student bar. She was out celebrating with a group of friends, having just passed the final exams for her nursing degree. He could see her long, long legs in clumpy heels and a violet mini dress that clung where it touched. He had thought that she must be a model, with her perfect figure and sculpted cheekbones, and offered to buy her a glass of wine. She had refused the drink but accepted his banter and danced with him instead. By the end of the night she had agreed to see him again. She'd been like a good luck charm too, that night. When they'd parted, he'd gone on to an all-night poker game and won nearly eleven grand. He'd bought her little diamond chip earrings as a thank you. They'd worked a treat. He smiled at the memory.

Her friends weren't impressed though. 'He's old enough to be your father, Jude.'

'Found yourself a sugar daddy?'

'Jude is thinking of specialising in geriatrics I see.'

She'd not taken any notice of any of them, and after a while, nor had he.

Poppy's conception had been a stupid mistake. He'd never thought for a moment that Jude would get pregnant, Sara never had, despite intervention, and he'd always supposed that it was his fault. He was too old for broken nights and nappies. He'd tried; of course he had, for a couple of weeks, but running two households that were only forty miles apart was fraught with the terror of exposure. Jude wanted him to be there all the time, clinging to him like a limpet. He'd invented more and more work away, and life settled down a bit. After a while, she had stopped mentioning marriage, or even buying a place together, and he thought they would be OK. That bloody kid got in the way all the time though;

it changed their relationship. Needy, needy, needy. Then just when he thought he was getting the old Jude back, the stupid cow got pregnant again.

The row had been extraordinarily fierce. Her arms crossed protectively across her belly, Jude had raged at him when he suggested that she should have an abortion, and that was when she dropped the bombshell about this pregnancy being twins. He'd had to get away before he was smothered in domesticity. He'd had this brilliant idea, and, always good at accents, had rung her from a call box in the middle of the night a couple of months later, pretending to be another man, a friend, and told her that Graham was dead, killed in a pile-up on the M40. She'd not been able to ring back either, which was just as well. He wasn't sure how he would've faked a funeral. Maybe she wasn't that keen on him, or maybe she'd seen through the lies. Whatever.

He wondered if she'd had the babies. She should've seen sense and got rid—she was only young, after all—plenty of time for her to have a family later. Your twenties was the age to have fun, not to wipe noses and change nappies. Anyway, it was different for women.

Graham was nowhere to be seen. Sara wandered round Casa Nuevo, picking up ornaments, and books, and memories. Even the sun-loungers and their cushions were for sale. 'TODO,' the signs blared. 'Everything.' The room attendants watched idly as she turned things over. Realistically, they weren't interested in this holidaymaker looking at the house contents. They were only interested in people who would buy the substantial things, the silver Mercedes in the garage, the surround sound system, and the state of the art kitchen. The odd trinket here and there didn't make any discernible difference. Summoning her courage, Sara drew herself up tall and approached the elegant young man lounging against the door in the dining room.

'Hola.'

'Yes, good morning.'

He didn't meet her eyes, still intent on the screen of his phone. His reply in English belittled her attempt at Spanish, labelled her a tourist. She refused to be put off.

'I can't come to the auction, but I'd like to buy this little picture please?'

'Auction is Wednesday.'

'Yes, I know that. I want to buy this today. How much?'

He sighed and took his time switching his phone off, his mouth in a bored sneer. He glanced at the little painting in her hands, an amateur thing of two children on the beach, just the typically sentimental sort of thing a middle-aged English woman would like.

'I don't know. Forty Euros?'

'Twenty.'

'Thirty-five.'

They settled on thirty, as they had both known they would. Sara counted the notes into the man's hand and asked for a receipt. He pretended he didn't understand her, but Sara stood her ground. There was no way she was going to let this objectionable man pocket her cash, and then say she'd stolen the picture. From behind her, a woman said something in Spanish, and he changed his stance, searching obediently for paper and pen.

'Sara. I told you it might be easier to have someone who spoke the language.' It was Ana.

'Thank you. I'm sure he understood what I meant, though. He was just being difficult. Weren't you?' Sara gave the man a cold stare. He shrugged.

'Your receipt, Senora.' He held it between two fingers disdainfully.

She tweaked it from his grasp and pocketed the bill without looking at it, but Ana stopped her. 'Let me see.' Sara passed it across. Casting a cursory glance, Ana waved the receipt angrily in the man's face, hissing something that even with her lack of Spanish, Sara could tell was threatening and probably questioning the man's parentage. Ana crumpled it up and gestured angrily, her voice loud and angry. Another man, older than the first, was summoned. This conversation was shorter. Ana thrust the crumpled note at him, and his expression darkened as he read it. He glared at the young man, who reddened. There was a brief, sharp exchange. The second man turned to Sara, smiling and apologetic.

'Senora, please accept my deepest apologies. My assistant here misunderstood you. We will of course, write you a bill of sale for you to take away with you. A lovely painting. Such good taste.'

A new document was produced. Wordlessly, Sara passed it to Ana, who nodded. The young man took the Euros from his back pocket and gave them to his boss. He glowered at Ana and sneered in Sara's direction.

'Ana, thank you so much. What did the first document say?'

'You don't need to know.'

'I do. It looked like a bona fide receipt.'

Over a glass of wine in Ana's dappled garden, Sara asked again.

'I'm presuming he wrote something rude.'

'Yes.'

'Don't tell me…something on the lines of "this old bag isn't even worth thirty euros".'

Ana looked torn between laughter and annoyance.

'Something like that.'

'Oh, the charm of some men. It's a good job you were there, or I would've handed it to customs and given them a good laugh at my expense, too.'

'His rudeness should get him fired.'

'Oh, hey, there's no harm done. I'm not going to let him upset me. My life's in far too much turmoil to let a little squirt like that get to me.'

'You've a problem? I thought you were on holiday?'

'My husband.' Sara couldn't explain and nor did she want to.

'Ah.'

Ana looked at Sara's tense profile as she stared out to sea.

'He has found someone else?'

'Something tedious of that nature. It's rather more complicated than that.'

'It usually is.'

Sara took another sip of her rosé, and smiled at Ana.

'But let's not talk about him. I've only got one more

day here. Why let it be spoiled? I'm going to lie in the sun and stare at the sea, while I have the opportunity.'

Ana put the rosé bottle back in the ice, and moved the bucket closer to Sara.

'Good idea. Live in the moment. Tomorrow is soon enough for problems, eh? Enjoy.'

Births, Deaths and Photos

Janet was busily packing Martha's things into a large tartan-printed zip-up laundry bag.

'The taxi will be outside in ten minutes. Have you got all the paperwork and pills and things you need?'

'Yes, Janet.'

Martha felt a bit like a schoolgirl with her headmistress. It was very strange, this role reversal. She waited to be asked whether she had brought a clean handkerchief.

'You didn't open your post. It's still here in this drawer.' Janet waved the envelopes admonishingly.

Martha shrugged. 'I forgot. I don't suppose there's anything urgent, there never usually is. I'll open it when we get home.'

Gloria insisted on giving her a hug. 'I'll miss you,' she said. 'We 'ad some fun, didn't we?' Martha smiled and nodded, and gave her the rest of the grapes and the magazines. 'Next time you're anywhere near Westgate, you drop in, yeah?' Martha assured her that she would, before Janet bustled her away.

The taxi driver was kind, helping the two women into the back seat of his Skoda, and putting Martha's bag into the boot.

'Bin in the wars, 'ave you, love?'

'A bit. I'm fine now.'

'Well done. That's the spirit.'

These roads needed resurfacing, Martha thought, cradling her plastered wrist against the bumpy ride. And whoever put speed bumps down a road where ill people were bound to travel was just a sadist. Wincing, she tried to ignore the ache.

'Here we are.'

From behind her sitting room curtains, Martha's next-door neighbour Doreen waved boisterously through the frilly lace, and mouthed something Martha couldn't quite make out. She nodded and smiled regardless, gestured vaguely with her left arm, which both felt and looked wrong, and picked her way carefully up the steps to the front door, leaving Janet to pay off the taxi. Her home felt empty and echoing after the noise and bustle of the hospital, and an icy finger of worry tickled the back of Martha's neck. In the kitchen, there was no sign of the mess she had left behind her, just five days before. Janet had seen to everything. As usual.

'Now, you sit down here, Mrs P.'

The old title slipped easily into place within the walls of the kitchen.

'I think after all this you can call me Martha, don't you?'

'We'll see. Old habits die hard. I'll put the kettle on.'

Janet dug in the tartan bag and brought out the bundle of envelopes, plonking them down on top of the mail that she'd picked up from the mat as they came in.

'Why don't you open your post?' She passed Martha the paper knife, and busied herself finding milk and pouring water into the cafetière.

Opening post with the wrong hand took more

concentration and effort than normal, and her progress through the pile was slow. The first few things were ordinary enough. A catalogue from Damart. That went straight in the bin, followed by a flyer for a new care home that was starting up a mile away, declaring 'dementia a specialty'.

'Oh, for goodness sake.'

'I hate all the junk mail we get these days. I asked the postman to stop delivering it once, but he said I had to fill in forms and I might miss things like registering to vote, so I didn't bother. I just put a bin by the front door now, sort the post there, that way I don't waste my time or my energy carrying rubbish down the hall.'

Martha laughed. 'Good idea. We'll have to set up something like that here, too.'

Janet put the coffee on the table and opening a little Tupperware box that she'd brought with her, she transferred some homemade fruitcake carefully onto a plate. She looked up as Martha made a weird sound at the back of her throat.

'Are you OK? Is it your wrist? Is it time for your painkillers? Should I ring for the doctor?'

In Martha's trembling hand were photocopies of three formal certificates. Birth certificates. They hadn't sunk in at first. Poppy Elizabeth Richards, daughter of Judith Richards, and Graham Edward Parker, born 03.04.2010. Keira Dilys Richards and Robert Jacob Richards both born on the same date, 12.12.2012, to Judith Richards, and Graham Edward Parker. Handwritten underneath 'father', the word 'deceased'.

Deceased.

The word made her head spin and she thought she was going to faint. Graham. Her Graham? Dead?

Monday, the last day of Jude's long weekend from work. Taking the kids to Weston had been a laugh, although getting them out of bed this morning had been like waking the dead. Robbie had whinged and dragged his feet all the way to the little primary school that the three of them attended.

'I'm tie-errred. I don't wanna go to schoooool.'

'Well, I'm afraid that's just tough, Robbie.' Jude pulled him relentlessly on. 'You'll feel better when you see your friends. You can tell them all about going to the seaside yesterday. Won't that be fun?' Oh God, she thought. I sound just like my mother. When did that happen?

At the school gate she handed an unwilling Robbie over to Mrs Saunders, who swept him along in her usual teasing manner, making him laugh. Hooray for smiley teaching assistants, thought Jude. She was fed up with being Big Bad Mummy. On the way back home, she mentally wrote the seemingly never-ending list of jobs that she had to cram in between now and half-past two, and wished she could clone herself. Turning the corner into her street, she met the postie.

'Anything for number 29?' she asked. 'I could save you a trip.' Jack riffled through the mail he was holding.

'There's this.' He proffered a plastic bag, printed with the apologies of the Royal Mail. 'It's been chewed by the franking machine, I'm afraid. Happens sometimes. Do you know whether everything's in

112

there? Were you expecting something?'

'No, and no.' Jude took the bag. It contained a brown envelope in two pieces and what seemed to be a ripped photo. 'Thanks.'

'There's an email address on the plastic bag if you want to chase something or make a claim.'

'Yeah, thanks, Jack.'

Heart thudding, she peered at the clear bag as she unlocked the house. It contained a now-crumpled photo, an old one, of a little boy in a hand-knitted jumper and grey school shorts, his socks pulled neatly up to his knees and his shoes polished to a gleam that even shone through the black and white picture. He was seated between a man and a woman—his parents, Jude guessed—who were neat and cheerful, smiling self-consciously at the camera. The man might not have been his father, she mused—in fact he might have been the child's Grandpa—he was much older than the woman. She turned the picture over. "Mr and Mrs Bernard Parker and their son Graham, July 1971."

Jude shut her eyes. Graham again. This time it was a picture from when he was just a little boy. She looked more closely at the image, wondering who on earth was doing this, and more to the point, why? He looked a perfectly ordinary kid—dressed in an old-fashioned way, of course, the picture was old—and she guessed he was probably a bit behind the times even then. Mr and Mrs Parker. So, these were his parents. Her children's other grandparents, she registered with surprise.

Like her own three, this was another child whose

father was much older than his mother; was that why Graham had been so anxious about being nearly fifty when Poppy was born? The couple looked ordinary. Kind, caring people with their dear little boy, who'd turned out not to be as upright as they'd hoped. Silently, Jude made a decision not to let her kids—particularly Robbie—inherit their father's slippery nature. The woman, his mother, was nice looking. She was familiar, somehow, too. Jude frowned at the photograph, trying to make her memory clearer, but whatever it was about the woman slipped elusively away. Maybe she looked like somebody on the TV; an actress from an old film, that would be it. Something to do with her hairstyle, probably, she looked like that woman in the old reruns of The Avengers that Jude had watched on Netflix. Yes, that was it.

Family Secrets

Janet was shocked.

'So you didn't even know your own son was dead? You poor woman. Fancy finding out like this. It's a disgrace.'

Martha was sobbing. 'We parted on such bad terms. We were both very upset—it was Bernard's funeral—and he said such awful things, Janet. The last thing he said to me was that I was a liar and he hated me. And now he's dead.' Another wave of sobbing overwhelmed her.

Janet rubbed Martha's shoulder consolingly. 'He didn't mean it. Of course he didn't mean it. He was young—he'd had a shock—every boy loves his mother.'

'Then why did he never come back?'

'Perhaps he was embarrassed. He was probably ashamed of himself?'

'For twenty-seven years?'

Janet blew her breath out, shaking her head. She held her hand out. 'Let me have a look at those forms.'

Martha passed the certificates over and Janet spread them on the table. Her tone became brisk and practical.

'So, let's see, Poppy will be seven, now, won't she, and the twins almost five? Do you still have the other picture?'

Martha was confused. She looked into the envelope the certificates had come in. 'There is no other picture.'

'The one you wouldn't let me throw away. The one that was behind your accident.'

Sighing, Martha pointed. 'It's in there.' Janet opened the end drawer in the pine dresser that sat in the corner of Martha's immaculate kitchen. At the top of the neat collection of cards and letters was the photograph of the children playing.

'"Poppy, Robbie and Keira in the park." It's these same children. They're Graham's children. You're a Grandma, Martha. How about that?' She smiled encouragingly at her friend.

Martha stared at Janet, her brain scrambled by the thought.

'But where are they?'

Janet read the certificates again.

'All born at Gloucester Royal. This looks a bit like Armscroft Park. That's got a play area. They could live near here. How about that?'

This started more tears. Janet got out her phone and started tapping on it.

'Who are you ringing?'

'I'm not. I'm searching for a Judith Richards on 192. I'm looking on the internet,' she added, seeing Martha's incomprehension. 'I can't get 4G here, though.' She crossed to the window and tried again. 'Nothing.'

Martha pulled herself together. She blew her nose awkwardly with the tissue in her left hand, screwed it up and shoved it in her pocket. 'We could use the computer at the library. If we put all four names in together, something might come up? A school play, or something? Every time we did a nativity, the local paper printed a picture with all the names. They might not do it these days, but it's worth a try…if we could find the

116

right school, we've got names and a photo.'

'And they'll think we're odd at least, or stalking at worst. There's got to be another way.'

'Well, we could go to the park. That park.' She indicated the photo. 'If we went at home time, it's a nice day, they might stop there after school. Graham used to like to do that.' She looked at the clock. 'If we went and sat on the benches by the swings, that'd be all right, wouldn't it? People will just see us as a couple of old ladies. Grandmas, even.'

She dabbed at her eyes and gave a hiccup of laughter through her tears. 'I might not have completely lost him, Janet. These children are my blood.'

'Their mother might not want to know you, though, Martha. You have to prepare yourself for that. She might not even know you exist.'

'I know that. I wouldn't blame her, but I'd never forgive myself if I didn't at least try…Nothing ventured, nothing gained. We've got almost an hour to get there. I'm going to smarten myself up. You organise a taxi.'

The Park

Dilys had dropped in to the terraced house where Jude and the kids were living. 'It's your day off, girl. What are you doing pushing a vacuum round? Get out and feel the sun on your skin.'

'Oh, Mum—this house is such a tip—I have to do something about it.'

'Are your children happy? Do they know you love them? Are their bellies full? Stop fussin'. Dust never killed anybody. Why don't we go and get ice cream and sit in the sun? You don't relax enough, Jude. I worry about you. You work, work, work, all the hours God sends. You're a human doin', not a human bein'. Chill. C'mon, give me that.'

Dilys took the vacuum from Jude and switched it off, winding the cable round the handle with determination.

'We'll go and get ourselves an ice cream, and maybe when the kids come out of school we'll get another and not tell them about the first one.' Jude started to laugh. 'That's better. And we'll take them to the park, let them run round and scream a bit. Kids don't get to do that enough any more. Do us all good. Frankly, there are days when I wish I could run about and scream a bit, too.'

It was quarter past three. Martha and Janet sat on a graffitied bench near the swings. Janet had bought them big whipped ice creams from the van that parked by the gate when the weather was good.

'I got one with chocolate sauce and one with strawberry. Which one do you want?'

It was nice, sitting in the sun, watching the families arrive.

'When I was a teacher, playtime was always my favourite part of the day,' confided Martha, licking a stray dribble of ice cream from the side of her hand. 'The other teachers didn't like playground duty, but I loved it; all that vitality, those wild emotions, the imagination those children had. Mind you, that was before computer games and wall-to-wall TV.'

Janet nudged her. 'Over there.' She crunched the last of the cone, and wiped her fingers and then her lips on a tissue.

'Where?'

'Just coming through the gate—see those two women—they've got a bunch of kids the right colour.'

'Janet.'

'Well, sorry. You know what I mean.'

Martha hastily finished her ice cream. 'Do I look all right?'

Secretly revelling in the sin of a illicit ice cream each, and burdened with reading bags and school jumpers, Dilys and Jude made their way slowly across the grass, choosing a shady spot to sit under a tree, while the exuberant children charged towards the swings.

'Keira. Be careful. Remember to hold on tight.'

Martha got to her feet.

'What are you doing?'

'I'm going to talk to them.'

'Who? The children? You can't. You'll get arrested.'

Martha looked at her in surprise. She hadn't thought about how it might seem to other people, a strange woman talking to playing kids. Times had changed. She wasn't giving up that easily.

'Well, I'll talk to their mother, then.'

As she got nearer, the women looked up.

'Oh, hello. Good afternoon. I—um—I'm sorry to bother you.'

'Martha?'

Martha had a moment of confusion. How did this woman know her name? The woman that she knew must be Judith Richards, laughed.

'This happens to me all the time. It's me, Martha, Jude, from the hospital, I'm a nurse, remember me?'

'Jude? Judith?'

'Well, yes, Judith, but only my mum calls me that, and then only when I'm in trouble.' She laughed, rising slightly to a kneel and sitting back on her feet. 'Are you feeling better, Martha? This is my mum, Dilys. This is Martha. She was one of my patients. Had a nasty fall, didn't you? I didn't expect to see you here. Isn't it a lovely day?'

This wasn't going the way Martha had envisaged. She smiled politely at the older woman with Jude.

'It's very nice to meet you. I'd shake your hand, but as you can see...' She waved at the plaster cast. 'Could I ask you a question, Jude? It's quite a personal question.'

'I guess so. I might not answer it though.'

'That's fair enough.' Martha could feel her heart fluttering in her chest. She swallowed nervously. 'Does the name Graham Parker mean anything to you?'

From her seat on the grass, Dilys snorted angrily.

'That man. He put her into this mess. Look at her. All the cares in the world on her shoulders and she's not even thirty.'

'Mum. Please.'

'Don't you try and deny it, girl. When was the last time you went out and had real fun? Tied to those kiddies, working the shifts nobody else wants? Skint all the time?'

Dilys subsided, muttering, under Martha's horrified gaze.

'Have you been sending me post, Jude?'

'No.' Jude hesitated. 'What kind of post?'

Something in the way she said it made Martha's mind leap ahead.

'Have you been GETTING strange post?'

'Yes—wait—who are you?'

'I'm Martha Parker.' She paused, fighting to stay calm. 'I'm Graham's mother.'

Gobsmacked, Jude sank back down onto the grass, her hands over her mouth.

'Someone has been sending me odd post about you. A photograph first. I didn't know you existed. I didn't know they...' she gazed at the laughing children, and she had to swallow hard before she could continue, 'I didn't know they existed. I haven't heard from Graham in more than twenty-five years. We had a row.'

Jude said nothing, staring at Martha. The silence

stretched on and on. Dilys took up the slack. 'Must've been one hell of a row.'

'It was. The last thing he said was that he hated me. And then this morning, I…I opened my post, and, and I saw…' unable to go on, she fumbled awkwardly in her bag and brought out the photocopies of the certificates. 'Deceased.' She whispered the word.

Jude froze, then snatched the papers from her hand. She glanced at them, her hands shaking as she read the names.

'Where the fuck did you get these?' Her voice cracked, every muscle tensed and for a moment, Martha was frightened that Jude would hit her. 'Judith Richards!' Dilys was outraged at her daughter's bad language. Jude ignored her mother, her eyes fixed on Martha.

'Someone sent them to me. And this, before.' She offered the picture of the children in the park. 'I didn't know what it meant. I didn't know who they were. I promise you, Jude, I'm telling you the truth.'

Dilys was on her feet. Uncertain where to go first, she shot Jude a fierce look and raised her hand in a "stop" gesture, before she put her arm round Martha's shoulders and steered her over to the bench where Janet was hovering anxiously. 'Now you just sit down. You're only just out of hospital.' Obediently. Martha sat and Dilys sat next to her, holding her good hand, murmuring nonsense, reassuring her. Martha had gone very white, and Dilys could feel the other woman shaking. She spoke to Janet across Martha. 'Did you know anything about this?'

'Not till this morning, no. I'm Janet. I'm—'

'She's my friend.'

Dilys patted Martha's hand again. 'We'll sort all this out. Don't you get upset, now.'

Jude walked slowly over to the three older women, her face stiff. She wiped the palm of her hand across her nose and mouth absently, before crouching in front of Martha.

'Listen to me, Martha. I HAVE been getting odd post about Graham. But I don't believe he's dead.'

Dilys gave one of her famous snorts.

'I don't. I didn't tell you, Mum, because I thought you'd erupt and I haven't got my head round it myself yet. But someone sent me this last week.'

She opened her bag and passed over the picture of Graham and Sara.

'On the back it says it was taken last year. But I got told he'd been killed when I was pregnant with Robbie and Keira. Really, I did. Someone rang me in the middle of the night, said he'd been in a crash, that he was dead, and the shock put me into an early labour. I spent more than a month on bed rest in hospital, Martha, and it was touch and go with the twins.' Her face was earnest. 'He didn't live with me, we weren't a very happy couple after Poppy was born, I was just so busy, and so exhausted, and only twenty-four, with three kids under three. I just tried to get on with my life.' She looked up at Martha, her face troubled. 'I'm sorry. I should've tried to find out more.'

'So he might not be dead?' Martha stared at this new picture in disbelief, her hands shaking. This middle-aged man—her Graham? Alive? She couldn't get her head around the new information, and tears were pouring unnoticed down her face.

'I don't know. He wasn't last year, anyway. And then this morning I got this.'

She passed Martha the torn black and white picture. Martha stared at it, hardly breathing, recognising an image that she hadn't seen for years. Where had this come from? Even she didn't have a copy of it any more. The three of them, together. She wondered if Jude would let her keep it for herself.

'He'd won a prize,' she said, blinking away tears.

Martha's voice was so quiet that they all had to lean in to catch her words. 'He'd won a prize at school for English. His teacher said he had the most wonderful imagination. A real gift for story telling, she said. She'd never met a child with such a grasp of the importance of a plot.'

Dilys's expression was reflected in Janet's face. The two women raised their eyebrows at each other. From the swings came a yell.

'Mu-u-um. Push me. Come and push me.'

Jude seemed to come to a decision. She handed the pictures to Janet, then stood up and held out her hand to Martha.

'Come and meet your grandchildren,' she said.

Micaela, Sara and the Cause of it All

Micaela was on the phone. 'So, update me. How's it going so far?'

'The second swathe of post has all been delivered and opened. Sara flew immediately to Alicante.'

'Wow. Really? She's a woman of action, isn't she? I might actually get some help there.'

'Yes. She bought a ticket for three days. Looked round the house, bought a picture of some sort for cash before the auction, and is due back this afternoon.'

'She didn't stay for the auction?'

'No. Obviously, I wasn't there, but sources tell me she only visited the house for half an hour. There was some sort of altercation. She spent the rest of the time sitting in the sun, drinking wine, I gather.'

'She sounds like a sensible woman. England is so dreary most of the year. What about the others? How's the old lady? Is she OK?'

'Yes, it wasn't anything too bad, a fall, I think. Martha was still in hospital with her broken wrist when the post arrived, so it was only opened when she got home at lunchtime on Monday. She might be old but clearly she's not to be messed with, either. She and her friend went straight to the park where the picture was taken, and sat and waited for the kids to come and play there after school.'

'That was a brave move.'

'It was. It worked too.'

'She's met up with Judith?'

'Yes, she has. That's two lots together.'

'Great. Half our work done for us already. How did the auction go?'

'Contents raised 22.000E. The house went for 501,000. Less commission and costs, we're about 65,000E short of our target.'

'What does Senor Garcia say?'

'He's not happy. After a good deal of negotiation, I've persuaded him to give us until the end of the month to raise the cash. We need about fifty-eight grand in UK pounds.'

'Right. Get part three couriered round. We need to act fast.'

'I'm on it.'

At Birmingham Airport, Wendy was waiting at Arrivals waving a huge piece of card that read 'We missed you, Senora Sara'. She was wearing a yellow fringed sombrero that was at odds with her tailored jacket.

Laughing, she waved as her friend came through the arrivals gate. 'Thought the least I could do was offer you a lift home after the fiasco with my passport. So, how was it? You've caught the sun.'

'It was beautiful. As beautiful as ever. Sad, though, somehow. It was strange to be there without Graham. Odd, you know?' Sara smiled at Wendy. 'Like saying goodbye to the place, and to a great chunk of my life with it.' She held up the paper-wrapped parcel that had been tucked under her arm. 'I bought a picture. Daft really. It's a sentimental thing, not at all like Graham's usual taste. In fact, I'm not even sure that I ever noticed it before.' She shook her head angrily at the emotion the visit had stirred in her. 'It's so stupid to get upset.'

'Of course it's not stupid. I'm glad you have something to remind you of the good times.' She linked Sara's elbow. 'Come on, let's get you home. Unless you'd rather go somewhere else. We could do something mindless, if you like. We could go to Ikea and mooch round the marketplace bit. Buy five thousand napkins and a bag of tea lights?'

Sara laughed. 'Let's go home. I'm dying for a real cup of tea.'

In the half-light of the noisome cellar, Graham was crying. He couldn't reach the planks nailed across the hole where the window had been to let in any more air, and the summer heat combined with the disgusting can in the corner was attracting flies; big lazy bluebottles that buzzed in his face but zipped out of the way when he batted at them. Self-pity and remorse had got to him. He was hot, thirsty and hungry and he was chained to the wall like a stray dog. That bloody Micaela better think of something soon or he'd die down here in the stinking heat, and nobody would ever find him. Bracing one leg on the earth floor, he tugged hard at the chain with both hands. The iron staple in the wall refused to give.

'Do you think I should report him as a missing person?'

Sara and Wendy were sitting in Sara's garden, and were half way down a bottle of cold Pinot Grigio. The patch of evening sun was shrinking and they had moved their chairs twice to keep up with it.

'No. He's up to something. Prob'ly got another 'nother woman. Forget the bastard.' Wendy slurred her words just a little, enough to make Sara suspect that she'd had a couple with Brian already, before she came back round to Sara.

'I can't just forget him. I'm still married to him. This time two weeks ago I hadn't even any idea that anything was wrong. I feel like I'm in limbo. I can't concentrate at work, I can't concentrate at home, my diet's gone to pot,' she raised the wine glass, 'and I'm drinking too much.'

'On the plus side, you've lost half a stone, I reckon. Every cloud, eh? Cheers.'

'Trust you.' Sara put the glass on the table and pulled her chair into the very last patch of sunlight. 'Seriously though, what should I do?'

On what he reckoned must be Friday morning, there was a crash at Graham's cellar door, as though someone had kicked it, hard. He shrank back into the corner, curling into a protective ball, trying to make himself look invisible. What if Garcia had found him?

'You are away from the door?'

The voice was female, with a strong Spanish lilt. Not Micaela's voice though.

'Yes.'

The door opened a crack and the tall woman slid through.

'More food and water for you. Christ.' She clapped one hand to her nose and mouth. 'It stinks in here.'

128

'When can I go? Is the house sold? Was it enough money? Is he still after my blood?'

'Not enough money, no. We have twelve more days stay of execution.'

Graham winced at her choice of words.

'Micaela works at it. Stay calm, stay quiet. Stay here. That was her instruction.'

The woman turned back to the door.

'Wait. Please. This chain…'

But she had gone.

Part Two

Pershore

A ring at the doorbell.
 'Mrs Sara Parker?'
 'Yes.'
 'Registered letter for you. Sign here please.'

A knock at the door.
 'Mrs Martha Parker?'
 'Yes.'
 'Registered letter for you. Sign here please'

A bang on the kitchen window.
 'Jude?'
 'Yeah?'
 'I signed for a delivery for you. Here you go.'
 'Cheers Ruth.'

Not that the recipients knew it, but the three letters were opened at exactly the same moment. Each delivery contained a note that said:

> *"Graham Edward Parker is in deep trouble.*
>
> *Please come to the café at No 8 Arts Centre, Pershore on Saturday, July 11th at 11am to discuss how you might help him.*
>
> *I will be sitting by the window, reading 'The Great Escape.'*
>
> *Please don't let him down, even if he has let you down.*
>
> *You could save his life."*

It was signed with one word. "Micaela."

Three women in three houses stared at three identical invitations, and all three of them reached for their phones simultaneously.

On the morning of Saturday, July 11th, Micaela got to the café at ten thirty-five. Someone was already sitting where she wanted to be, where she'd told the others to meet her. Shit—she should have thought of that—who knew it got so busy in a little town like this on a Saturday morning? She had only chosen Pershore because it was halfway between Stratford and Gloucester, and this café had seemed to be a place where they could meet unnoticed. She bought a coffee and sat as close to the other table as she could, where she could still keep an eye out of the window. She thought they'd be early, if they came at all. Fumbling in her bag, she brought out her copy of *The Great Escape* and propped it conspicuously against the little posy of flowers in a bud vase that sat in the centre of the table, before realising the book was far too heavy. Catching the flowers as they tipped, she swore under her breath, righted the vase, opened the book so its spine cracked and put it face down on the tablecloth, leaving the title clearly visible. Adjusting her chair slightly, she watched the glass foyer intently, worried she might miss one of them arriving. A man's voice made her jump.

'The Great Escape, eh? Marvellous book. Loved the film too. Steve McQueen, eh? What a man. Mind if I join you?'

The man was tall, with a big nose and a wispy beard.

131

He was loud, oily and confident, certain of his allure. Micaela recognised him as a huntin', shootin', fishin' sort of Englishman of the very worst type. He was already unloading his refreshments on to her table. She picked up his coffee cup and put it firmly back on his tray.

'I'm sorry, I'm waiting for some friends.'

'Well, I'll only be five minutes. This place gets so crowded on a Saturday morning. I promise I'll go when your friends arrive.'

He winked at her. He actually winked. She hated him on sight. He had some of the same overconfident attitude that Graham had when she first met him, Micaela realised. She'd mistaken it then for charm, but later come to recognise it was just egotism. This conceited fool thought she was just using an excuse. He started to pull out a chair. She hooked the leg of it with her ankle and jerked it out of his hand.

'Tough. You should have got here earlier. Go sit over there.' She pointed to another table where a fat man was working his way through a large slice of chocolate cake with steady determination. Two huge scones and a pot of cream sat waiting as second course.

'I'm sure there's no need to be quite so rude.' Sniffily, the man turned away, sending her a venomous look over his shoulder as he enquired grumpily of the other seat. The fat man nodded with boisterous enthusiasm, and started chatting with his mouth full, spraying cake and crumbs all over the table as he spoke. Micaela smiled in quiet satisfaction and turned back to the window.

In the big supermarket car park, Jude turned to Martha.

'Are you sure you're ready for this?'

From the Panda's back seat, Dilys fidgeted and tutted. 'This is a fool's errand. You mark my words. You'll regret it, both of you. It'll be a scam. '

Janet nudged her new friend, deciding that a little distraction would probably be helpful.

'I haven't been to Pershore for years and years. Shall we have a little walk down by the river? We could all meet up in, what, an hour? Do you think an hour will be enough?'

'To be fleeced by some crook? Bound to be.'

'Mum.'

Dilys pursed her lips. 'Well, don't say I didn't warn you.'

'Yes, OK, I hear you. But this isn't helping any of us, is it? Martha and I will go and meet this Micaela woman and see what she has to say. We're not committing to anything, we're just going to listen, that's right, isn't it Martha?'

Martha nodded, her eyes fixed straight ahead. Her emotions were wound so tightly that she daredn't speak. Arm in arm, the two women set off to find the café.

'This is a fool's errand. I've said it before and I'll say it again.' Dilys put her hands in her cardigan pockets and turned to Janet. 'Which way's the river then?'

In the town square, Sara and Wendy got out of the BMW.

'You needn't come in with me.'

'I will, though. I'll sit nearby, in case you need help.

133

Just drop something as a signal and I'll come and be a long-lost friend and get you out of there. Don't sign anything.'

'As if.'

As they waited to cross the road, neither of them took much notice of the black car with Spanish number plates that cruised by, searching for a parking spot.

Micaela held the book up in front of her face as the old woman with the plaster cast—his mother—and the tall black girl—the mother of his children—came through the door together. Her mouth was dry, although she'd rehearsed and rehearsed the words she had to say all night. The girl—Jude—spotted the book, and pointed Micaela out to her elderly companion. Not making eye contact, and not smiling, they picked their way carefully through the tables of chatting shoppers.

'Micaela?'

'Yes. Hello.' She shook hands with both of them, hesitating awkwardly and swopping hands to shake Martha's left hand ineffectually. 'Thank you so much for coming. Please sit down. Can I get you a coffee? This might take some time.'

Unwillingly, grudgingly, they sat. Micaela stood up, ready to go to the counter. As she did so, she saw Sara come in, so she waved and held up the book. Jude and Martha looked at each other, bewildered. Another woman? Jude suddenly recognised her from the pool photograph, although Martha, she realised, hadn't worked out who the smart blonde woman was. Sara looked equally taken aback, and hesitated. Micaela hurried over, speaking urgently, and the elegant woman came over to their table.

'I gather you are as much in the dark about this meeting as I am?' She had recognised the Spanish woman she thought of as "the fake bride," now standing at the counter, waiting for service, but she had no idea who these other two were.

The three of them laid their invitations on the table and waited in silence. Jude held Martha's hand, and squeezed it reassuringly. Sara looked at her own neat manicure, avoiding eye contact with the others while she waited. She wasn't sure she could swallow coffee and cake. Out of the corner of her eye, she saw Wendy join the back of the queue for coffee, just as Micaela was paying at the front. Bearing drinks and flapjacks on a loaded tray, Micaela hurried to join them and sat down.

'Thank you for coming, all of you. I know this is extremely odd, but we all have something in common.'

'Graham?' Jude's tone was bitter, almost sarcastic. Martha winced to hear such hatred in the young woman's voice. She let go of Jude's hand gently, and fiddled with the handle of her coffee cup instead, drawing her fingers round and round the curve of the handle.

'Graham, yes. And he is having big trouble.'

In her stress, Micaela's Spanish accent was apparent.

'And just who the hell ARE you?' Sara's voice was practically a hiss.

Micaela turned to her. 'Please. I can explain to all of you together, OK?'

135

They nodded.

Wendy sat down at a table where Sara could see her. She exchanged a few words with the two men she'd helped out in the coffee queue as they passed her on their way to a table upstairs. Honestly, fancy nobody in an Arts Centre speaking a second language. She was quite proud of the ease with which she'd picked up on 'Dos cafés solo, por favor' and helped the holidaymakers get their drinks. Spanish had always been her favourite subject at school. And now, here was Sara, clever Sara, who went to Spain every year, admitting she hadn't bothered to learn the language. Sometimes Wendy felt quite superior.

'OK.' Micaela put down the first photo, the one that Jude had received a copy of only a few days earlier. 'This is Graham Edward Parker, age eight, with his mother, Mrs Martha Parker,' she nodded at Martha, 'and his stepfather, Mr Bernard Parker, who he loves very dearly. At Bernard's funeral, Graham learned he was not Bernard's natural son, and rowed most furiously with his mother, and she hasn't seen him since. That was in 1990. In 1992, he married Sara Jane Kendal,' a nod to Sara this time, 'and they set up their home in Shottery, near Stratford-upon-Avon.'

Martha gaped at Sara, astounded. So Jude wasn't his wife? Sara had never been mentioned before—although wait—was she the pool woman? Martha's head spun trying to assimilate this new information. Micaela held up a hand to stay her questions, and carried on.

'Graham buys and sells foreign property, timeshares, offices, commercial buildings, so he works away from home a lot, but he and Sara appear to have a good marriage. In 1997, he literally charms the pants off a twenty-year-old intern called Micaela Fernandez, and persuades her to marry him.'

She touched her throat with both hands, identifying herself as this foolish twenty-year-old. 'I came to England, to Oxford, in the snow, all on my own, and went through what I believed to be a strange English wedding.' She placed a copy of her wedding photo on the table. 'I find out only weeks ago that it was something called a Humanist wedding, and not legally binding. More just a statement of affection than a real contract of marriage. I swear I had no idea he was already married, or that what I went through wasn't the truth.'

Jude went to interrupt, but Micaela held up her hand again. 'Please, let me finish. I know this is difficult to believe. He worked away a lot. We didn't see much of each other. I was living in Spain and working long hours, and Graham was often away, working all around the world.'

Sara started to cry, softly.

'Then after a few years, he suddenly seemed much richer, and he bought a house in Calpe. We rented it out as a holiday home, and barely used it ourselves. He used to wine and dine clients there sometimes, and also let it out to friends. I never lived there. I prefer the city. When he had big contracts coming up, he used to encourage me to go and stay with my brother Luis in

137

Madrid. He said he couldn't concentrate on business if I was around.' She shot an embarrassed glance at Sara. 'I think that's maybe when you came for your holidays.'

She put the picture of Sara and Graham by the pool on top of the other two. 'But I go ahead too quickly. In 2010, Graham meets a beautiful girl in a bar and falls in love again. They are years apart in age, but that doesn't matter. They see each other most often, and this girl, Judith,' here Micaela gestured towards Jude, who had her elbows on the table and her fingertips lightly on her brow, 'believes that Graham loves her. That year, she gets pregnant, and this isn't in Graham's plan. Poppy their daughter is born, and Graham begins to visit less often.'

Jude looked at the table. Martha put her hand over Jude's, and squeezed it. Sara felt sick. A baby. The longing rose up in her chest until she could hardly breathe. Micaela was still talking.

'In 2012, when Jude is again five and a half months pregnant, Graham rings her in the middle of the night, using a strange accent that you call—uh—Ge-ordie?' She stumbled over the pronunciation, making the word musical, 'and tells her there has been a terrible crash on the M40, and Graham is dead. The shock puts Jude into early labour, and she nearly loses her babies.'

Sara's hand flew to her mouth. 'The bastard.' She paused, the word dropping its significance. 'BabIES?'

Silently Micaela placed photocopies of the birth certificates on the table. 'Poppy, his eldest daughter. Robbie and Keira. Graham's twins.'

'However, Jude's been managing without him ever

since. As have you, Martha. And you and I—' here she indicated Sara, 'have been sharing him, unknowing.'

There was a stunned silence.

'But how the hell did he afford to do all this?'

'He's a gambler, Sara. An addict, playing cards and dice for serious stakes. It has all been going his way for years, but now he has got himself in big, big trouble. He lost, an enormous loss, to the wrong people. And they want their money back. Immediately.'

'And if they don't get it?'

Micaela drew her finger eloquently across her throat. Upstairs in the gallery, the two Spanish men were watching intently. At Micaela's throat slitting gesture, one of them turned to the other and laughed. The first man shook his head, his eyes never leaving Micaela's face. He wanted to see how these other women reacted.

There was a shocked pause while they took this in. Sara shook her head in disbelief.

'Surely that sort of thing only happens in cheap movies? How much does he actually owe?'

Micaela smiled grimly.

'He DID owe more than a million Euros, but the sale of everything he owned has brought that down immensely. The house in Calpe, a little flat in Zante that nobody but Graham knew about and all the contents of them both, plus various concealed money has brought the debt right down. But the final amount, sixty-five thousand Euros, must be paid by the end of the month or the debt will double. And Graham will be killed.'

'What can we do?'

'How much is sixty-five thousand Euros?'

'Where is he?'

'He's safe for now. He hides, in Spain. Is just less than sixty thousand pounds. We must decide if we can find enough money to save him. And whether you want to help save him. Whether you believe me that he deserves to be saved.'

'Of course we must.' Tears were pouring down Martha's face, and her voice was louder than she intended. People sitting at the nearby tables turned to stare.

'Shhh.'

'I don't care. Let them look. We have to save him. He's my son.' She turned desperately to Sara. 'He's your husband.'

'He's a liar and a fraud and a cheat and a bigamist.' Bitterest of all was the thought of the babies. Three babies. Somehow, that was the worst betrayal of all.

'Yes. He's all that too. But we can't just let him be murdered.'

Jude had been silent throughout. Now she spoke up.

'I have no money. It's as simple as that. I've three kids to support on my own, I barely make ends meet as it is. I'm sorry, but what can I do?' Her voice was tense and wavery with emotion. She spread her hands out in despair. 'What can I do?'

Sara shook her head and looked at the table.

'Nothing. You shouldn't have to do anything. He got himself into this mess, and changed the pattern of your life callously. And mine. And yours—Martha?' She hesitated over the old woman's name, uncertain if she'd recalled it correctly, or whether she had the right to call her by her first name at all. 'Leaving you alone for all these years. He told me his parents were both dead. I'm so sorry.'

Martha stared at Micaela. 'He's my son. I can sell something, anything, everything.' She began struggling with her plastered hand to pull the wedding ring from her finger, tugging at it when it stuck on her knuckle.

The old woman's distress got to all of them, and as one woman they reached to stop her.

'We need a plan. We must work out what to do. Is everyone agreed that we ought to save him, even if he is a lying, cheating, bastard?' Micaela was urgent, more aware than any of them just how swiftly Garcia would act if he didn't get his money.

'Yes.' Martha didn't hesitate.

'Yes. But I don't know what I can do. I'm completely skint.'

There was a pause. They looked at Sara. The noise in the café rose and fell, as outside their tense little collective, the world turned regardless. A woman laughed, and a toddler threw an impressive tantrum. Silently, the other woman watched Sara. Everything rested on her decision. They had to work together. A full minute passed before she spoke.

'Yes. If only to prove that we can rise above what he's done to us.' She sighed deeply. 'That we won't sink to his level. That we won't be his victims. That we matter, we aren't just his puppets.' Her mouth tasted as acid as the tone of the words she spat out. She knew her face was ugly with contempt.

141

'Right. Agreed.' Martha turned to Micaela. 'How are we going to do this?'

'We can't just rush into it. We've got one chance to do this and it has to be right. Just selling a few precious things isn't the way.'

Sara's face suddenly creased with horror as realisation hit. Jude turned to her in concern.

'What's the matter?'

' Oh, my God, my house. OUR house. Will I lose it? What if they decide to take it?'

Micaela looked at Sara in concern. 'It's a real risk, yes. You must see your solicitor and find out whose name is on the deeds. You might be able to do something.'

'I have a nest egg.' It was Martha, quiet and dignified. She seemed to have aged in front of their eyes; her shoulders had slumped and her head was down. 'I was saving it as Graham's inheritance. Every year he didn't come back, I put some money aside. It's not enough, but it'll go a long way towards it.'

They looked at her. Her sadness was tangible. All that love, all that hope, crushed by her stupid, greedy, ungrateful son.

'I'll check how much is in it. I'll have to go to the bank, make arrangements to withdraw it. They won't be open now 'til Monday.' Her despair was tangible, and the other women couldn't look at her.

Eventually, when Micaela spoke, her voice was quiet. 'So, we need to think, yes? Sara, find out about your house. Martha, you will go to the bank, yes? I will tell Senor Garcia that we are working to find a solution.'

It was agreed that they would meet at Martha's house on Monday, with their ideas.

Wendy gave the others a couple of minutes after they left, so that she didn't look like she was obviously with Sara. As she gathered her bag and the newspaper she'd been using as cover, she saw the two men coming down the stairs. 'Buenas vacaciones!' They can't have heard her though, ignoring her as they hurried to the door. Ah well. She made for the square and Sara's blue BMW.

The Duplicity of the Man

Sitting in the permanent twilight of the cellar, Graham was thinking about Micaela again. She had been absolutely magnetic with her dark eyes and huge smile, full of enthusiasm for life and eager for fun. He'd met her just after a fantastic win at the Casino Medi in Benidorm, and he had money to burn. He'd driven her up into the hills for an evening picnic, and made love to her in the twilight. God, she was gorgeous. He couldn't believe his luck. On the spur of the moment, fired by oxytocin and starlight, he'd gone down on one knee and proposed to her. He was over the moon when she'd said yes. Sara hadn't even crossed his mind. Sara, his wife, human abacus, counting days, measuring hormone levels, dictating when he could and couldn't touch her, desperate for a baby. Boring, tedious Sara, who used to be up for a laugh. So much for that.

So, instead, he'd persuaded Micaela to come to Oxford one snowy winter weekend, and they'd had a Humanist marriage. Micaela had never been to an English wedding. She was charmed by the idea that they could be married in such a personal, private little ceremony in a snowy hotel garden, using their own vows, the thin gold band glinting in the watery winter sunlight. She was frozen, he remembered, in that sexy dress, but she'd never stopped smiling and laughing all day. She'd been so happy. In the evening he had said he had to pop out for a while, charmed her, sweet-talked away her petulance, promising flowers and a surprise when he returned.

He'd nipped into the John Radcliffe to see Sara
before he went to the card game. Tearful, hopeful Sara,
lying as still as she could, her mind somewhere else as
she used every ounce of her will to encourage the
implanted embryos to stay in her body; for them to love
her as she loved them already. It was all so depressing.
She was barely listening to him at all as he tried to make
conversation. After ten minutes, he'd told her she
needed to rest, kissed her forehead blithely and shot off
to play Blackjack for a couple of hours.

His second wedding night was a bit of a fiasco really.
He'd been on a winning streak, so he'd stayed at the
tables for just a bit too long. When he left, it was 4am
and pitch dark. Micaela had been crying and wouldn't
look at him, her fiery Spanish temper rising like a
tsunami of fury. She had started hitting him, demanding
to know who the other woman was. He told her there
was nobody else, that he'd only been playing cards, but
instead of placating her, this drove her into an even
greater frenzy.

'Bastardo.'

He'd had to pay the hotel for the lamp and the
telephone that she'd ripped from the wall and hurled at
him. Odd, really. You'd have thought she'd have been
pleased he won.

It seemed an endlessly long drive back to Gloucester.
Martha was silent, and Jude was preoccupied. Sitting
cramped in the back of Jude's elderly and rather sticky,
Fiat Panda, the other two women sat in silent

contemplation. Janet and Dilys had enjoyed their walk and got to know each other well. They'd found they had a lot in common, and they shared a healthy cynicism about Graham: Janet explaining about the lack of evidence around the house; the locked bedroom she was never encouraged to go in; the photo albums put away in the loft—Dilys talking of her daughter's infatuation with a man that she, Dilys, had seen through within the first five minutes of meeting him.

'"He grows on you, Mum," she said to me. I told her so did athlete's foot, but you could get treatment for that. And you should have seen his face, when Poppy was born. Thundercloud wasn't in it. He was all smiles when he came to see Jude, but did I ever see him play with that poor little child? Never. And then of course, he "died",' she made inverted commas in the air with her fingers, 'so Jude never got a penny of child maintenance. It's not even that she married him. No widow's pension, no insurance money, nothin'.' Janet and Dilys had tutted, and shaken their heads at the duplicity of the man.

They'd tried to ask about the meeting, but neither Jude nor Martha wanted to talk.

'I'm tired,' said Martha. 'I think I've rather overdone it today. I just need to go home and get an early night.'

'It's only just three o'clock.'

'One of the benefits of living alone. You can do what you want, when you want.'

'Have you eaten, Martha? Taken your tablets?'

'Oh, don't fuss, Janet.'

It was unlike Martha to be so abrupt. Dilys and Janet

146

exchanged looks.

'I'm sorry. That was very rude of me. I'm just tired, that's all.'

'It's fine. I understand.' Despite her concerns about leaving her alone, Janet made Martha a cup of tea and then, respecting the other's need for solitude, went back to her own flat.

On the way back to Stratford-on-Avon, Wendy had tried to get Sara to open up about the meeting.

"I recognised that Micaela,' she said. 'But who were the other two? The black girl and the old woman? Who were they?'

Sara really, really didn't want to tell her. This whole sordid mess was just so humiliating, so frightening, that she didn't have the words.'

'Other people he's screwed over. It's really complicated, Wend. My head's pounding. Can we just leave it for now? I need to get my brain into gear, and frankly, all I want to do right now is get home and take some painkillers.' She could sense from her friend's stiff posture that Wendy was offended. She risked glance in her direction. 'Sorry Wend. I really appreciate you coming with me. I will tell you, I promise, but I need to sort it all out myself, first. Is that OK?'

'Of course, Sara.' Wendy's voice was just a bit chilly. 'Take as long as you like. I'm pleased I could be there to support you in your hour of need.' She nearly added 'It's in my nature. I helped out two Spanish tourists in the café this morning,' but decided to keep that to herself. If Sara couldn't be bothered to talk to her,

Wendy certainly wasn't going to chat.

Oh Christ, that's all I need, St Wendy the Martyr, thought Sara. Forcing a smile, she touched Wendy's arm lightly. 'I knew you'd understand.'

It was Sunday morning. Janet rang Martha's doorbell at ten o'clock as she let herself in and was shocked to find her still in her nightclothes, her hair in a mess and her distracted air that of a woman twenty years older.

Stating the obvious had never been Janet's method. She took off her jacket and went upstairs to the bathroom, turning on the hot tap and pouring in Radox.

'I've run you a nice bath, Martha. I reckon if we put your arm in a couple of plastic bags, you can rest it on the side and it won't get wet. Come on.'

Her tone was firm. Obediently, Martha sat by the side of the bath in her nightie while Janet taped the bag to her arm.

'I know you can manage, but I'll just be outside the door. You might want some help getting out.'

She pulled the door to and listened for the sound of Martha climbing into the bath and lying back with a sigh. Reckoning she had ten minutes, Janet nipped into Martha's bedroom and pulled things straight, noting the much-thumped and slightly damp pillow, and the twisted sheets. She decided to change the bed and opening the airing cupboard door on the landing, called, 'Are you OK in there?'

'Mmm.'

'Lovely. You take your time. Give me a shout when

you want to get out.'

Might as well do a thorough job. Deftly she stripped the bed and flipped the mattress over with a grunt. Tucking in the fresh sheets, she noticed the book on the bedside cabinet; some kind of accounts book, with page after page of notes and figures in Martha's small neat handwriting; teacher's handwriting, thought Janet with a smile. She was about to pick it up when there was a noise from the bathroom.

'Janet. Can you please—?'

'Coming.'

Sara had had a sleepless night too. She'd been going through one of the rank of filing cabinets in the spare room that Graham used as his office when he was at home. There was no system in the cabinet, no order at all. Not even hanging files to keep the documents apart. His preferred method of filing seemed to be to open the drawer, chuck the papers in, slam the drawer and hope that some magic filing fairy would sort it all out in the night. The floor of the office was now covered with heaps of paper, as she desperately tried to restore some order, but some of the documents were going back several years. She was only on the first drawer of the first cabinet, and there were five cabinets. She was tearing her hair in despair.

There was a knock at the front door. Great. That was all she needed. Bloody God Squad with their daft magazines. She ignored it, but the knock came again. It wouldn't be Wendy—she always used the back door— in fact they'd cut a gate between their two back gardens for ease rather than trudging all the way round the front of the semi-detached house they occupied between them. On second thoughts, though, perhaps it WAS Wendy. She'd clearly taken offence yesterday when Sara hadn't given her the full explanation of the meeting—she hadn't even popped round in the evening to see if everything was OK. Normally, she would've done. Oh, God, she wasn't ready to eat humble pie. She really hoped it wasn't Wendy. She peeped cautiously out of the window, feeling slightly foolish. The black Audi looked vaguely familiar, as did the top of the tall man's head as he waited outside the front door. Some sixth sense made him look up, and he spotted her and waved before she could duck away.

'Hi, Sara.'

Matt. She'd have to let him in, she supposed. If only for five minutes. Checking in the landing mirror for smudges of yesterday's mascara under her eyes, and wiping a black shadow away with her thumb, she scooted down the stairs and opened the front door with a rigid smile.

'Matt. This is a surprise.'

'I've been popping by now and again since you left the office, Sara, this is the first time I've caught you home. I was worried about you. How are things? Can I do anything?'

About to say no, Sara suddenly changed her mind. Matt had an analytical brain. There was a sea of paperwork up there. Throwing caution to the wind, she opened the door wider.

'How long have you got?'

Building Bridges and Climbing Frames

It was too nice to stay inside and fret, especially as there was absolutely nothing she could do to help raise money. Instead, Jude made a heap of peanut butter sandwiches and packed a backpack.

'Who wants to go on a picnic?' There was a chorus of approval.

'Can that old lady come?'

'What old lady?'

'The park lady. The nice one with the smiles and the poorly arm.'

'Martha?'

'Yeah. She likes us. She might buy us ice cream.'

'Robbie.'

'What?' He gave his best wide-eyed-innocent grin.

'Never mind.'

Jude thought about it. It might work, and it would be nice to get to know her, see how she was. Yesterday had seemed to take its toll on the old woman though; she had got back into Jude's car looking frail and much older than when she'd got out of it only a little over an hour earlier. Frowning, Jude switched off her inner nurse. She reached for the phone. 'I could ask her.'

Robbie clapped his hands, his infectious grin making her smile, as it always did. Just for a second the word 'manipulative' flitted through her mind, as Janet answered. 'Good morning.'

For a second, Jude wasn't sure she had the right number. 'I was hoping to speak to Mrs Martha Parker, please.'

'Who's calling?'

'My name's Jude. Judith Richards.'

'Oh, hi Jude. It's me, Janet. She's in the bath just at the moment.'

'Right. Well, never mind, it's not urgent. It was just a thought.'

'Do you need her to call you back?'

'No. We were going to go for a picnic, that's all. We wondered if she might like to come with us?'

Janet lowered her voice.

'Between you and me, Jude, she had a really bad night. I don't think she's up to it.'

'Right. That's understandable.' Jude wondered how much Janet knew. She couldn't quite work out the relationship between these two women, and they hadn't offered an explanation, either.

'Why don't you all drop in afterwards though? There's a big garden here—the children could play outside—I could make us all some tea. It would do her good to see you. She loves children. She was the head of a big junior school before she retired, you know.'

'I didn't.' Jude paused. Did she really want to do this? She dismissed her thoughts about how the kids would behave—or more specifically, how Robbie would behave. Martha was their grandmother. She ought to see them, get to know them better. If Robbie was his usual monstrous self, it was better she realised that sooner rather than later. And anyway, it would be nice to see her again, see where she lived, see if she could work out just what had gone wrong between

Graham and his mother. She made up her mind. 'Yeah, OK, that'd be nice. I'll ring you a bit later to let you know our timings, would that be all right?'

'Yep, fine.' Mentally, Janet was already thinking about butterfly cakes and jelly, remembering the birthday parties she'd made for her own boys, years before. She put the phone down.

Half an hour later, Janet and Martha were sitting in the sparkling kitchen with a pot of coffee and a pile of crisp bacon sandwiches. Martha seemed a bit brighter, restored by the combination of a hot bath and someone to talk with.

'There are three things you need when you've had an upset,' declared Janet, 'and eleven o'clock is too early for a whisky, so we'll have to make do with caffeine instead.'

'Three things?'

'Food that's an indulgence, a stimulating drink and friendship.'

Martha looked away while she pulled herself together. 'I'm a silly old fool, Janet. I've let myself dwell in Cloud Cuckoo Land for far too long. Graham isn't a good man. He isn't even a nice man. But he's still my son and he's in desperate danger. I have to help him, even if he doesn't care about anyone other than himself. I have to.' Her eyes were searching Janet's face, willing her to recognise her inner turmoil, to tell her that she was doing the right thing.

Janet nodded. 'I can understand that.'

'Last night I couldn't help thinking, it's ridiculous

that I rattle round in this great big house, all on my own, just in case he comes back. He's never coming back, Janet, I know that now, and after yesterday's revelations, I'm not even sure that I'd want him to. I'm thinking that maybe I might sell up and buy myself something smaller, something more practical. This is a house for a family, not one old woman on her own. I might even move to one of those little retirement complexes that they're always advertising.'

Janet was astounded.

'What? You always chuck those brochures in the bin. You've told me what you think about corralling old folk into ghettoes. What did you call them? "God's Waiting Rooms." You can't.'

'Look at me.' Martha raised her arm. 'I can't even get out of the bath on my own.'

'You've got a broken wrist, not a walking frame. You'd hate it. Move if you must, but not into one of those.'

Martha sipped her coffee and said nothing. Janet passed her the plate.

'Have a sandwich. Go on, you need to eat'. A battle of wills threatened, but Martha backed down, and took the smallest sandwich on the plate. 'Thank you.'

'They're coming for tea, by the way.'

'Who?'

'Your grandchildren. Jude rang to see how you were, and I invited them for tea.'

'When?'

'Today. This afternoon. About three o'clock. Lovely garden for children to play in, this.'

'You invited them?'

'On your behalf, of course.'

'Are you trying to manipulate me, Janet Reeves?'

'Only a bit, Mrs P.'

Martha narrowed her eyes at Janet's mock subservience. Janet just laughed.

'I know Graham seems to have become a bit of a swine, Martha, but that's hardly your fault, is it? You gave him a wonderful family life, it was up to him to react the way he did, and anything he's done since Bernard's funeral has been entirely off his own bat. You've got another chance at family now, with this sparky, caring girl and her lovely children. You grab that with both hands. Not many people get a second go at happiness.'

Martha thought how Bernard had said something in much the same vein, almost fifty years ago. "I know I'm a bit stuck in my ways, Martha," he'd said. "I'm not a bright young thing like you, but I love you, and I'll love Graham as if he was my own son. You'll never want for anything, I'll keep you both safe, I promise. We can be so very happy if we just try. Let's go for it. Martha, will you marry me?"

He'd stuck to his words. They'd had a wonderful life together; the three of them, until death had stolen Bernard from her, and Bernard's stupid sister had stolen Graham, with those thoughtless words. Barbara must be long dead herself now, Martha supposed. All that venom. Stupid woman. She squared her shoulders and sat up straighter. 'I've had it firmly drilled into me that I'm too old to go in the loft, Janet, but *you* haven't been told to stay off ladders. There's Lego, and jigsaws and all sorts up there. We could maybe get a few of Graham's old toys down? They'll have novelty value for these children, if nothing else.'

Janet cleared the coffee things, pleased to hear Martha sounding more like her old pre-accident self. 'No problem. I'll be up that ladder like a ten-year-old. Let's have some fun.'

In the park, the kids were playing tag. Robbie, as usual, was getting grumpy that he couldn't catch Poppy, and so instead he tackled Keira with some force, pushing her over in his frustration. She went flying across the grass, landing full length and sitting up bawling, her pride damaged even if her body was fine.

Jude opened her eyes and sat up. It was too much to hope that she could just lie in the sun for five minutes. 'Robbie. That was mean. Come here right now.'

Robbie danced away, but his sister Poppy grabbed him. A slapping, twisting fight began between them. Jude got to her feet and jogged over, separating them. 'You, stand here, and you, stand here. Do not move. Stay there.'

She picked up a howling Keira and set her on her feet between the other two. 'Right. Now is this the way to have a nice time? Is it?'

They all avoided her eye.

'Robbie. What do you say to Keira??

'S'rry.'

His voice was hardly audible, but Jude let it go.

'Poppy, I know you were trying to help, but grabbing

your brother hard probably wasn't very nice for him was it?'

'No.'

'So what do you say?'

'Sorry.'

'And now what do we do?'

They all looked at her, awkwardly.

'Group hug?'

'Group hug.'

It probably wasn't the friendliest hug in the world, but it pulled them all back into their family unit. Jude was convinced they could survive anything, if they just stuck together.

'Good. So, that's all over, yes?'

'Yes, Mum.' A dutiful chorus in one sing-song tone.

'Good. Help me out here, I can't quite remember. Is there anyone here who likes ice-cream?'

Back at Martha's house, Janet was cooking up a storm.

'They're not vegetarian are they?'

'No idea. Why?'

'I thought I'd make some sausage rolls.'

It was Martha's turn to laugh.

'They're children, Janet. They want crisps and fizzy drinks and chocolate and cake. Our job is to sneak some real food in there somewhere without them noticing. I wouldn't worry about preparing an afternoon buffet for the Queen.'

Janet, busy cutting 'wings' in the buns to turn them into butterfly cakes just smiled and reached for the chocolate butter icing.

C for Chaos

Matt looked at the mounds of chaotic paperwork all over the office floor.

'Blimey. I'd never have imagined that you…' He stopped short realising he was sounding a bit judgmental.

'This isn't my mess. This is my dear husband's inner sanctum. Although I'm not entirely certain he IS my husband any more.'

The last sentence was under her breath, almost as if she hadn't been aware of mentioning it out loud. Matt raised an eyebrow, but said nothing.

'I had no idea that he just filed things under "C" for "Chaos". I've got to find some important documents.'

'What are you looking for?'

'Oh, you know, little things. House deeds, bank statements, that kind of thing—'

'Can I help?'

Sara looked at him gratefully. 'I thought you'd never ask. Seriously though, Matt, that would be great. Just look at this.' She opened a random drawer and he saw just what she meant. The mound of paperwork slithered as she pulled the drawer out hard.

'Oh God. No clues at all?'

Sara shook her head. Her voice was level but she was clenching and unclenching one hand rapidly. 'I can't find any sort of order. At first, I thought it was just as if he'd put the papers in until the first drawer was full and then started on the next one, but it's not even as simple as that. By the muddled dates on the documents, I think he just walked in here, pulled open a drawer, any drawer, in any filing cabinet, then just chucked the stuff in and walked away. I'm finding all manner of things.'

She snatched a handful of documents out of the nearest drawer and held up a catalogue for garden equipment, a red gas bill and a map of Alicante, at random. 'It's going to take forever.'

'Right.' Matt took off his jacket and rolled up his sleeves. 'Any chance of a coffee?'

By the time Sara got back upstairs with two mugs of instant, Matt had pushed back the furniture and laid sheets of A4 that he'd obviously taken out of the printer on the floor. Each was marked boldly with a year.

'The way I see it; it's easier to do this in two stages. First, we'll just separate the stuff into years.' The labels started with 2017 and went backwards to 2010. 'I've guessed maybe things might go back further, but we haven't floor space. So the plan is, we put pre-2010 stuff in an empty drawer and do that lot when we've bundled the later stuff up. Then when these years are sorted, we can go through the early ones and sort that paperwork into types. It'll take a while, but it'll put things in a system.' He took a swig of coffee and brushed aside her thanks. 'Let's go for it. I always love a challenge.'

Sara was pleased he didn't ask any questions, and they worked pretty much silently for the best part of an hour. Then Matt cleared his throat. 'Where IS Graham,

Sara? Is everything OK?' His tone was casual, but Sara sensed he was serious.

She didn't look up, and there was a long moment before she cleared her throat and replied to him. 'Honestly? I don't know. On either count. I haven't heard from him for a couple of weeks, and I've been getting some very odd mail. He's in trouble, Matt. Money trouble, and I'm frightened.'

'Hence hunting for the house deeds?'

'Yes. I'm scared I'm going to come home to the bailiffs banging on the door and taking everything I have. I had no idea he had debts.' She blew her nose angrily. 'I feel like I don't know him any more, like maybe I never knew him.'

Wisely, Matt kept his mouth shut, sensing he might find out more by letting Sara ramble on.

'I met his mother for the first time yesterday. He'd told me his parents were dead. I've been married to him for twenty-six years, and I've only just met his mother.' The laugh that emerged might have been a sob, but Matt kept his eyes on the paper he was sorting, aware of her turmoil. 'Do you know who else I met, Matt? The mother of his children.' Her voice was bitter.

At this, Matt DID look up. She held his shocked gaze.

'Oh yes, Graham has children. He forgot to tell me, it seems.'

'But they must be in their thirties, I guess? He was married before, maybe?'

'You'd hope so wouldn't you? But no, it's nothing as simple as that. Graham, it appears, has three children.

Poppy is seven and Robbie and Keira are twins. Four-and-a-half year old twins. What does that make me, I wonder. Aunty? Wicked stepmother? Fool?'

'I don't know what to say. Oh shit, Sara.'

'Yes, that seems to cover it nicely, I'd say. Oh, SHIT.'

Breaking eye contact, she started to sort the pages again with an urgency that bordered on manic fury. 'I need to find the house deeds. Thank God the business is in my name alone. I might lose my house, but that bastard's not taking my business. I need those deeds.'

He nodded. 'You do. I'm starting on the next cabinet.'

'Thanks, Matt. Thanks for listening.'

Living in a Movie Script

Micaela, sorting her washing, wondered what the other three women were doing. She'd done her bit, and now it was over to them to come to a decision about how they could help raise the cash. Vaguely, she wondered about Graham, how was he managing? Her cousin Elena had said it was pretty disgusting in the cellar, but they couldn't risk setting him free, or Garcia finding Graham before the debt was paid. As soon as it was possible, she had to get him out of the country, and fast. The further she could get him from Spain the better. She was getting too old for air steward work, anyway. A nice desk job in the airport would suit her fine, regular hours, a comfortable chair and best of all, no sick bags.

Maybe, now that everything was out in the open, Graham would realise that she was his best option. She could perhaps even persuade him to go to Australia or New Zealand with her. She was sure she could get a two-year transfer with her job and then they could get married properly, as soon as he and Sara were divorced, as they surely must be now. Micaela had seen hurt in Sara's eyes, but also a fierce, burning contempt. She wouldn't take him back, that was for certain. Micaela knew she was being foolish, but she loved Graham, rat or not.

It had been horrible, that night he'd banged on her door, almost a month ago now. Like all regular aircrew, she had a couple of rooms that she rented from a friend for stopovers. She always stayed there, it was close to the airport and although basic, had the best hot shower in Spain. She'd just got thankfully into bed after a particularly trying few days of almost non-stop shuttling back and forth, when there was a terrific hammering on the front door. She sat bolt upright, clutching the covers with one hand and scrabbling for the light switch with the other.

'Who is it?'

'Me. Let me in, Mic, for Christ's sake.'

She'd pulled the bolt back and almost been bowled over by the speed he'd barged through the door, slamming it behind him, banging the bolts home and pulling a chair across to wedge under the door handle. Then he'd pulled all the blinds down and turned off all the main lights, pulling her into the windowless bathroom and shutting the door before turning a light on. It had been like being transported into a Jason Bourne film.

'What the hell's happened? Graham? Are you OK?' He was shaking and panic was coming off him in waves.

'It's Garcia. I can't pay him.'

'Garcia?'

It had all come out. Graham had been playing cards. For days on end.

'I kept thinking that in the next hand my luck would turn. It always has done before. But instead it got worse and worse. Oh Christ, what am I going to do?'

He had sunk to the floor, his back to the wall, his face in his hands. He looked old, and ill and terrified.

163

'He'll kill me.'

It was a flat statement.

'Who will? This Garcia? Who is he?'

'He runs the casino. Lots of casinos. Most of the casinos in Spain, in fact. And he's trouble, Mic. Big trouble. He'll kill me if I can't pay.'

'I've got some savings, I can help you.'

Graham laughed. There was no sound of humour.

'I doubt you could get anywhere near.'

'Why? How much do you owe?'

He shook his head.

'How much, Graham?'

She'd never forget the expression on his face.

'Just over a million Euros'

'What? Fuck.' She couldn't comprehend such a huge amount.

'Oh Christ. What am I going to do? What am I going to do?'

He was rocking back and forth, his arms wrapped round his head like a child. Desperately, Micaela dropped to a crouch and tried to take his hands, willing him to calm down, to look at her, to tell her it was all a joke. His expression told her otherwise. She tried to stay calm.

'Can't you reason with him?'

'Ha. Nobody reasons with Garcia. They do what he says or suffer the consequences. I reckon most folk that cross him just disappear.' He momentarily put his hands up to his head again, as if he were trying to order his thoughts, his face an image of dread. 'There's a lot of new building in Spain, most of it done by Garcia's

164

companies. An awful lot of concrete foundations, you know? Plenty of people end up being pillars of the community, know what I mean? Literally, in this case.'

'Shit.' She wracked her brains. 'What about the house?'

'What?'

'Would he give you time to sell the house in Calpe?'

'No.'

'He might. You could ask him.'

'Not a hope.'

'What if I talked to him?'

'He'd laugh at you. And then he'd send his men to follow you back here and kill us both. It's taken me an hour and a half to get across town—I kept doubling back, in case I was being followed—I don't think his men are after me yet, but they can't be far behind.'

Micaela sat on the edge of the bath and stared at him, her mind whirling. This WAS a movie script. Henchmen, for Christ's sake? He was babbling, not making any sense. First things first. 'We've got to get you to a safe place.'

'He'll find me.'

'He won't. Get up. I've got an idea. I need to make some phone calls. Are you sure you weren't followed here?'

'I don't think so.'

'Right. Get a shower. You stink.'

It was true. Graham was dirty, dishevelled and stank of sweat and whisky from days on end in the casino. When he emerged from the shower, a pale green towel knotted round his waist, she threw her crumpled uniform at him. 'Put this on.'

He stared at her, confused.

'I'm dressing as a trolley dolly?'

'Air steward. You are.' The correction was automatic.

'It won't fit.'

'It'll fit enough to get to the car. And it'll look good enough to get you to Calpe, in the car, in the middle of the night. Do it.' Shaking, he'd done as she asked. He looked ridiculous, but it was their best chance.

She'd already put her spare uniform on. 'Hat and lipstick.'

'What?'

'Hat and lipstick. We're never without them. If they're looking for you, they're looking for a man. They'll ignore two "trolley dollies" like us.' She spat out the phrase like poison.

Shakily, Graham drew on circus clown lips. The hat was the right size, at least.

'Right.' She passed him a shoulder bag. 'Your own shoes will have to do. Keep talking about what a prick Keith is.'

'What?'

'Keith. The Lothario of all pilots everywhere. We all hate him. Come on.'

In the car, they headed not towards the coast, as Graham had expected, but to the airport.

'I thought you said we were going to Calpe. We're not going to the house, are we? He knows about the house.'

She shook her head. 'Air stewards driving to and

from the airport is the normal thing. So that's what we do. There's a flight due in at five. We drive to the airport, park, wait, and when the next lot of crew disembark and leave, we leave too. Then we drive to Calpe—but no, not to the house—somewhere else. We can spend the time in the car park planning how we can raise the money. We will do this, Graham, you must have no doubt about that. Have faith. It will be all right. I will make it all right.'

Her plan had worked. Arriving in Calpe as the morning bustle started to awaken the town, Micaela had taken him to her father's cousin Elena. Their Spanish was too rapid for Graham to follow but he had caught the gist of it.

'This is Graham. He's in big trouble. He's a shit of the first degree, but I love him. He needs to hide for a while.' Elena had goggled at this strange man dressed in drag, but begrudgingly agreed to Micaela's plea.

When he caught the word 'bodega' his hopes rose, maybe they were taking him to a bar? It was only as the started to descend the dark steps that he remembered it meant 'cellar', too.

'Stay here. I'm going to get you some supplies.'

'And some clothes?' He indicated his bare legs. 'I can't stay like this.' He'd smudged the lipstick off as best as he could and the lower part of his face was alarmingly streaked in red, like blood.

'Yes, OK. I'll be about an hour. Don't make any noise.'

She'd left him with food, water, some trousers and a T-shirt much to his relief, some wet wipes and a couple of blankets, promising to be back. And then she'd steeled all her courage and gone to see Senor Garcia.

'I need six months to raise the money.'

'No.' His tone was cold, dismissive. Micaela's heart was pounding, but she kept her voice and her gaze steady. He was just a man, she kept telling herself. She could negotiate with him, persuade him to give her some time.

'Just one month, then. You'll get your money, but we need to find it. The house will raise a lot.'

'I doubt it will raise enough.'

'No, but it'll raise more than you'd get if you just kill him now. I can do this, senor. Give me some time.' She'd stood her ground, not looking away from his cold gaze. Eventually, after the longest silence, he'd nodded, just once, curtly. She tried not to show her relief.

He'd given her one month. Back in Calpe, sobbing pathetically, the truth had poured out of Graham. It was like an endless stream. He told her how he'd abandoned his mother at his supposed father's funeral, how he had another wife. A real wife. How her own marriage was a sham. And the final blow had been the girl, Jude, and her children. He'd faked his own death and abandoned his family.

She'd nearly taken him straight back to Garcia right there and then.

'I'm so sorry,' he'd sobbed, 'I'm so sorry, Mic.'

They were so close to the final figure now. Surely these other wronged women would help her to save him? She knew he'd done some dreadful things, but Micaela couldn't imagine life without him. She could change him. She knew she could. There were organisations to help gamblers, weren't there? It was an addiction, like alcohol or smoking. She would help him. They could do this together.

A noise in the street made her look out of the window. Four floors below a traffic warden was being given grief by a couple of smartly-dressed men. One of them was tearing a parking ticket in half while he shouted at the warden, the other was lighting a cigarette. The traffic warden's words drifted up. 'Look pal, I don't care. See that sign? Permit holders only. If you've got no permit, you can't park here.' The black Mercedes roared away, leaving the warden shaking his head and writing something in his book.

Micaela smiled. Sunday morning in London. What did the Brits call them? Jobsworths, that was it.

Family Life and Filing Cabinets

Janet was amazed just how much noise three children could make, she'd forgotten, after all these years. She wondered if her Australian grandchildren were as noisy as this. Worse, probably—they had all that space to fill with noise. Martha had got her to look in the shed at the end of the garden, where she'd found an array of battered toys from years ago. A metal blue and red scooter was proving very popular, as were several heavy yellow Tonka trucks and a slightly rusty pogo stick.

'Are you sure these are safe?' Janet asked.

'Probably not. But that's what childhood's about, isn't it, learning to handle risk. And they'll be on grass, and their mother's a nurse. It'll be fine. Stop worrying.' Some of the colour had returned to Martha's complexion and the years were falling off her. She winked at her friend. 'This was a great idea. Thanks Janet.'

Slowly, all of the filing cabinets were emptying. They'd underestimated the length of time that Graham had been using this filing system; some of these documents went right back into the late 1990s. Red bills seemed to be prolific.

'Didn't you ever pay a bill on time?'

'Don't look at me. I thought he was paying them. It seems as if he always waited for a final demand. Lots of people do that, you know.'

'I guess so.'

'Just because you pay things immediately, doesn't mean everyone does.'

'Do you?'

'Well, yes, but we aren't talking about me here.'

'We're talking about your husband, though. Didn't you ever get suspicious of the number of official letters he got?'

'Well, maybe at first, but he told me he was involved with buying and selling lots of properties, so I thought they were for those. That's what he told me. So after a while I used to just pop them in here on his desk and leave it to him.'

'Ah.'

'Yes. OK. NOW I realise that was stupid. No need to rub it in.'

'Sorry. What does he do, in property?'

'Nothing.'

'Sorry?'

'Nothing. He told me lies. He used to be a property broker, years ago, when we first got married. He never actually sold the timeshares himself, but he organised things for the companies that do. He acquired office blocks, and cheap land, all sorts of things like that. I thought he was still doing that, but it would seem not. He's been living as a semi-professional gambler for the last twenty-odd years, and I never guessed. Each time he went away, I just presumed he'd got another new timeshare to promote. It turns out it was a poker tournament or a baccarat game.'

'And now he's losing instead of winning?'

'Oh yes. And losing big time. To real sharks.'

'Oh Sara.'

'How much more paper is there?'

'Two more drawers.'

'Keep going.'

Eventually it was all in heaps.

'We're never going to sort all this out in one day.'

'No. You decide, Sara. Do we start with this year and work backwards, or the earliest stuff and work forwards?'

'God knows. Any sign of the house deeds?'

'Not that I saw. Wouldn't they be lodged with your solicitor, though? That's what usually happens, I think.'

'Oh God, why didn't I think of that? Micaela said that too, I think. In all the turmoil I just forgot.' Shit, shit, shit, she thought, I'm losing it. Focus, Sara, focus. 'I'm in such a state, my brain isn't functioning clearly. Of course they must be. Do you suppose I can ring them on a Sunday?' She looked at her watch. It was nearly four. They'd been sorting papers for more than six hours.

'Shouldn't think it'll do any good. You'd be better off calling first thing in the morning. Come on, now we've got this far, let's see if we can reduce this to just the essential stuff. Got a bin bag? In fact, got a roll of bin bags?'

Jude watched her kids play and turned to Martha. 'Thanks so much for this. They're having a great time.'

'I'm so sorry about Graham, Jude. The way that he's treated you is despicable. I'm so ashamed of him.'

Jude reached for her hand.

172

'Don't be. You didn't know. You had no idea.'

'He was such a lovely child. Nobody would believe he'd turn out like this; doing these dreadful things.'

She swallowed hard and then gave Jude a brittle smile. 'Can I read them a story before we have some tea? It might calm them down a bit first.'

'Good plan.'

'I've still got lots of books from my teaching days. Mystery, violence, or princesses?'

Jude laughed. 'I get enough violence and princesses in my everyday life. Let's have a mystery.'

'We've got that in our real life too, at the moment.'

'True. Can we save him, Martha?' Her steady gaze demanded an honest answer

'I don't know. But we'll try our best, Jude. We have to try.'

Shaking the Piggy Banks

Monday afternoon, and the planned meeting time had arrived. Two cars, Sara's big silvery-blue BMW and Micaela's little red Seat Ibiza, pulled up on the drive outside Martha's house. Jude was already there, virtually, in the form of her mother, Dilys.

'Jude's told me everything. She's at work. The kids are all going to friends after school today, so I can help.'

Dilys settled herself into the most comfortable of Martha's chairs, assessing the room critically. The heavy velvet drapes, the G-Plan units, the Parker Knoll suite. She ran a tentative hand over the silk cushion as she tucked it into the small of her back. 'You have a very nice house, Mrs Parker.'

'Martha, please.'

Dilys nodded. 'Terrible thing your son did to you.'

'And to Jude.'

'Yes.' She stared at Martha, her face unreadable. 'Sure he's worth savin'?'

Martha's expression told Dilys everything she wanted to know. She smiled grimly. 'I get it. He's not worth savin', but he's your flesh and blood. I get that.' She looked down and picked up the tea that Janet had brought in. 'I got sons. It's what us mothers have to do.'

The air was tense until there was a knock at the door. Sara Parker and a very tall man in a dark suit.

'Hi. This is Matt Lincoln, we work together.' Dilys's eyebrows rose but she said nothing. 'Matt's been helping me sort through some legal stuff.'

They sat silently on either end of the sofa, waiting. It was a relief when the doorbell went again and Micaela came in.

The six of them drew a collective breath. Martha, recognising her position as hostess, cleared her throat.

'All right, who wants to start?'

Micaela spoke first.

'Graham is still safe, but he's not in a good way. His nerves are very worn, and he's getting unpredictable. In the night, my cousin has added some extra locks to the outside of the cellar where he is hiding, in case he tries to escape.'

'He's a prisoner?' Martha was horrified.

'He has to be. If he does something foolish and gets out, Garcia's men will find him. He's not acting reasonably. I have Graham's phone charger, too. I couldn't afford for Garcia to trace any calls he might make.'

'Could he do that?' Sara was fascinated, if horrified.

'I wouldn't put anything past him. He'll have some of the Policia in his camp, I'm sure. Somehow, he'd manage to find Graham.'

'Right. Let's get our cards on the table.' Martha winced at Dilys's choice of words. 'My Jude has nothin'. I have nothin'. We can offer encouragement and support, but nothin' else.' Dilys sat back, content that she'd done all Graham deserved.

'I understand that. We all do. Jude's got the roughest deal of all of us.'

Even as she said it, Sara knew she was lying. They'd all got a rough deal. Looking at Martha's stricken face, she couldn't begin to imagine what the poor woman was going through. At least Jude had got three beautiful children from Graham, more than she, Sara, had ever had. And look at Micaela, why was she humiliating herself like this? Sara wondered why, how, Micaela had ever stuck by this man that none of them really knew at all.

'Sara has been on to her solicitor and found that her home is in danger,' Matt spoke out. 'She and Graham are registered as tenants in common, so they can't take the house from her, but they can exert pressure to make her sell and give them Graham's half of the monies raised.'

Martha closed her eyes and shook her head. 'That can't happen. My savings aren't anywhere near enough, either. I'll sell my house.'

Janet held Martha's hand and squeezed it.

'This is no good.' Micaela was desperate. 'That could take months. We need the money by the end of THIS month. Does nobody have any money? Real money? What about your car, Sara? It's almost new. An expensive car like that would raise some cash.'

Sara shook her head. 'No, I can't, it's leased. It belongs to the company, anyway, not to me. It's only mine for two years.' She paused. 'I suppose I could cash in my pension, but why the hell should I? What will I live on when it's gone?'

'Then you can sell your house, maybe?'

'Micaela, perhaps you don't understand. I don't WANT to sell my house. This man has cheated us all. At the moment, I'm sorry, but right at this moment I don't really care much if he lives or he dies—my marriage is a sham—my whole life for the past twenty-five years is a sham. I don't even know who I am any more. I'm certainly not the woman who celebrated her silver wedding anniversary last year.' She burst into tears. Awkwardly, Matt touched her arm, desperate to comfort her but not knowing if he should. Dilys solved the problem by plonking her wide hips between them and enveloping Sara in a hug.

'You cry it out, girl. That man's caused nothin' but tears.' She glared at Micaela, as if it was all her fault.

Micaela clenched her jaw and her fists. 'I'm sorry. I'm sorry for all of us, but we have to do something. Didn't you ever have a good time with Graham? Didn't he ever make you all feel special? Didn't you love him, once? We can't just turn him over to be murdered.'

Matt cleared his throat. 'Well, look, this isn't really any of my business, but Sara and I have been trying to sort out Graham's paperwork, which is, I have to say, in as much a mess as the rest of his life. I've found a few bits of paper that suggest he sometimes took goods in lieu of gambling debts in his favour. I'm not suggesting that you part with your favourite things, but do any of you have little things that you could maybe offer up as having some value? Things you wouldn't miss? Perhaps Garcia would do the same thing—accept objects instead of cash?'

'Sixty thousand pounds worth of pretty ornaments?' Micaela was dismissive. 'Garcia won't be tempted by that.'

'At least Matt's trying to help.' Sara, much recovered

and half-suffocated, rose to his defence from the depths of Dilys's embrace. 'Let's all keep looking.'

It was agreed that they would get in touch by Wednesday. It felt like a time-bomb was ticking down.

That night, Micaela phoned Elena.

'How is he?'

'He is like a raging bull. He needs you here to calm him, Micaela. He's started to make too much noise. He has been here more than two weeks now. You said just a few days. Someone will hear him. He crashes on the door and shouts for help. Word will get about. If Garcia finds out that I've been helping to hide Graham, I could be in danger too. This isn't fair on me.'

'No. No, you're right. Tell him I will be there on Friday. Tell him he must keep quiet just another couple of days, maybe? Can you not slip him something to make him sleepy? Just to calm him down?'

Elena promised to see what she could do.

Matt was sleeping in Sara's spare room for a couple of days. He and Sara spent every waking hour outside work in Graham's office. To counteract gossip, he always parked a couple of streets away, and they arrived at, and left work separately. Sara kept waiting for Wendy to come bouncing into her kitchen and find them together but it didn't happen. 'She must've been more offended than I realised', Sara thought guiltily. 'I ought to go round and say "hey, how's it going?" ' The idea of nosy Wendy adding her own particular brand of chumminess to the situation was more than Sara was prepared to handle just now. She put off banging on Wendy's door, and concentrated on the paperwork instead. Slowly they were establishing order.

'I'm going to have to bill your husband for my time, you know,' Matt joked.

Sara thought he might just be serious. 'My soon-to-be ex-husband, you mean.' She straightened up. 'I mean it. This isn't something we can ever get past. When I rang Helen about the house deeds, I spoke to her about Graham, a bit. I've started divorce proceedings.' Helen was the company lawyer.

'What grounds?'

'Take your pick. Desertion, bigamy, other women, illegitimate children? My solicitor said it wasn't likely that any of it would be contested. It'll probably go through fairly quickly.' She sighed. 'To be honest, Matt, it'll be a relief. We've been living on borrowed time for years, I think, living two separate lives and only really playing at being married when we met up. All this chaos,' she threw her arms wide, encompassing the office around her, 'is because when he's here physically, he's somewhere else mentally. It's no way to live. We'll get him safe, and then I'll get shot of him for good. He's not really been mine for years. Who knows what other women he's been entangled with over time, anyway? We're just the other three key players that Micaela is aware of, me, Martha and Jude. Well, if Micaela wants him, she's welcome to him, and the best of luck to her. I've had enough.'

Matt was reading something, distracted and only half listening. He took a deep breath. 'Sara, this might do it.'

179

'What?' The world seemed to stop. He was staring at the scrap of paper he was holding, a scrap which shook in his normally steady hand.

'He took a painting as a debt. A painting by an important Spanish artist. If we can find it, we might just find the money. Have you heard of an artist called Sorrolla?' Hearing her declaration of independence, Matt was even keener than before to rid Sara of Graham speedily.

She shook her head. 'No. Oh my God, Matt, where is it? How do we find out? Is it valuable? Is it valuable ENOUGH? What does it look like?'

'Ah.' Matt attempted to keep his tone light. 'That's the tricky bit. It just says "Sorolla oil painting, estimated value to be well above the outstanding debt of 35000 euros" and both Graham's signature and another I can't read. Then something in Spanish. Can you read Spanish?'

'No. We could try Google translate?' She fetched her iPad. Matt tapped the sentence in. 'Acepto este cuadro pintura total y definitivo de la deuda. Esta pintura ahora pertenece a Graham Parker.'

'I accept this painting as total and definitive payment of the debt. This picture now belongs to Graham Parker.'

'That's it? It's legally his?'

'Yup. They've both signed it, look.' She took the screen gingerly, as though shaking it would make the words vanish.

'35000 euros would be a major step towards the debt. - But what if it's at the Spanish house? It will have

180

already been sold.'

'Well, there's not much we can do about it, if it has. This is as good a straw to clutch at as any other. Give me your iPad back a minute. Let's see if we can get a few clues as to what it might look like.'

He searched for Sorolla. 'Here we go. Joaquin Sorolla y Bastida. They called him the Master of Light. That's a clue then.' He read on. 'Oh God, this'll make it tricky.'

'What?'

'Well, he was fairly prolific, it seems. Hundreds and hundreds of paintings.' There was a pause. 'Values are rising on his paintings, apparently. There have been a couple of major exhibitions.'

'Oh.' Sara couldn't breathe, she couldn't think, she couldn't let herself HOPE…Her fingers tingled with pins and needles and she could hear her heart thudding. Matt kept scrolling through screens on the computer.

'He signed them though. Look.' Matt enlarged the corner of an image he'd pulled up. 'Does this ring any bells? Have you seen this on anything? Try and remember, Sara—it's quite a clear signature, look.'

'No. I can't—' She bit her lip, trying to recall all the pictures in Calpe. '—mostly it was just prints, I think.'

At the same moment, they looked up at the prints on the study walls. Hopper's "Nighthawks," Monet's "Poppies" and Degas' "Absinthe Drinker" were not what they were looking for.

'Not any of these either, then.'

'No.' Sara got to her feet. 'Come on.'

They walked carefully through every room in the

house, examining the pictures. Most of them were prints, with a couple of watercolours by local artists on the landing. In Sara's bedroom, Matt was careful not to look at the bed.

'What's that?' He pointed at a square flat parcel, wrapped in brown paper, that was leaning against the wall down by a basket-loom chair.

'What? Oh that? That's just a picture that I bought last week, in Spain…at the auction.' Her mouth went dry. 'Well, before the auction, really. I couldn't bring myself to stay and watch my memories being sold off. It won't be this.'

As she was speaking, Sara was unwrapping the parcel, quickly, carefully, her heart hammering in her throat. She had to keep swallowing and her fingers scrabbled at the tape. It was ridiculous to even consider that this could be the painting to save them. To be honest, she couldn't quite remember what it was. A beach, maybe? It was probably done by one of those artists you see lined up along the promenade in Benidorm. She pushed back the final layer of bubblewrap.

The painting was small, and showed a young naked child paddling, with an older girl, dressed in a white shift, standing nearby. The sunlight was bright, and you got the feeling of a breeze and chilly water; the younger child's shoulders were slightly hunched and one hand was clenched up close to his face. They gazed at it silently, neither wishing to voice that vital question.

'That's rather lovely.'

'Yes. Is it the Sorolla, though?'

182

'Could be. The light's right.' Matt scrolled rapidly through the images on the tablet. He could feel a fluttering pulse in his neck as he searched, flicking through the multitude of pictures faster and faster. Then he stopped. 'Oh my God.'

He turned the screen round. The identical painting faced her.

'It might be a copy.'

'It might be. Do you have any idea how you get a painting authenticated?'

'Not a clue. Find an expert?'

'Where do we do that?'

'We could try at the National Gallery, I guess.'

'Right. Good plan. Fancy a trip to London, then?'

'It can't be as simple as that. Anyway, we can't both take a day out of the office at the same time.'

'Why not? I've some holiday owing and you've taken time out with some unknown problem, everyone knows that. They're not expecting you in. In fact, they're running a book on what the matter is.'

'Are they? Bastards.' She looked at him and narrowed her eyes.

'Actually,' Matt looked slightly shifty, 'I've got very good odds on you getting a divorce.'

Sara started to laugh. There was a touch of hysteria in her tone.

'Sara?'

'Do you know what I paid for that painting, Matt? Thirty euros. If I'd have waited for the auction, someone might have recognised it. It might have sold for its true value. We could have been spared all this chaos.'

'And you'd still be in the dark about Graham.'

'That too.'

He took a deep breath and tried to sound casual. 'Sara, when this is all sorted out, would you come to dinner with me?'

She smiled at him and didn't hesitate. 'Yes please.'

'Great.' He held out his hand. 'Pass me the laptop— we need to send an email and some photographs of this.' His dark eyes sparkled at her. 'Let's get this show on the road.'

Drugs and Worry

Graham was feeling laid back and mellow. The woman, Elena, she was called, had taken pity on him, and brought him a great big plate of chicken and rice. She'd brought another bucket too and wincing, had covered the other one with a piece of wood. He thanked her, and tucked in ravenously. He was famished, and it was a large helping, he guessed that was why he felt so sleepy. He might as well have a little snooze, after all, there was nothing else to do. He curled up in the two nasty rugs, and made himself as comfortable as he could. Distant sounds faded as he surrendered himself to sleep.

Elena was on the phone again. 'Micaela, I did as you said. I put three of the sleeping pills into some chicken. He is fast asleep.'

'Three?'

'Si. Just to be sure.'

'Is that safe?'

'I have taken two before now. Three is not so different. He is a big man. Anyway, a sleep will do him good. He rages in that cellar from morning till night. I hear him moving around. This way we both get a little peace, yes?'

It was only for a few more days. Reluctantly, Micaela agreed that keeping Graham sedated was probably a good idea.

Wednesday morning, and Sara and Matt stood on the

steps of the National Gallery, lost in their own little bubble of anxiety. The train from Warwick Parkway had only taken an hour and a half, and they were early for their meeting with the art guy. London seethed around them, taxis and buses and pigeons and crowds. Wrapped in many layers of tissue and bubble wrap, the little oil painting was safely tucked away in Sara's leather holdall.

'Ready?' Matt took Sara's free hand. 'Let's go.'

Thursday, 2.06pm
Text from Sara to Micaela.

Hi. Ask S. Garcia if he would be interested in authenticated Joaquin Sorolla oil, valued by the National Gallery to be worth between 75k-100k. Paperwork can be supplied. S

2.55pm
Text from Mic to Sara.

Garcia very interested. He is something of an art collector. Please send image.

3.10pm
Text from Sara to Micaela.

Attached image of cert. of authenticity. Demand written promise of cancellation of debt and safe passage for G. on transfer of painting and monies from sale of property and contents before picture revealed.

3.12pm
Micaela to Sara

You're playing hardball.

3.13pm
Sara to Mic

You bet. Ask him.

Eight o'clock, Thursday evening and Martha's phone rang. Wondering who it might be at this hour, she answered warily. She was not in the mood for scammers this evening. 'Hello?'

'Martha, good evening. It's Sara. I know it's late, but I've got some news. If I pick you up in an hour, can I take you to Jude's house? She can't get a babysitter and we need to talk as a group.'

'Yes, if it's important.'

'It is. I'm sorry it's late.'

'No problem. Just because I'm getting on a bit doesn't mean I'm always tucked up in bed at eight in the evening, you know. I'm quite a night owl, really.'

'Yes? Great. I'll set off now then.'

Martha put the phone down, wondering what had happened. She meant it about staying up. She'd dismissed the help the hospital had offered after the first night, when a well-meaning woman had tried to persuade her into nightclothes at seven fifteen in the evening.

'But I don't ever go to bed before midnight.'

'Well, you could put your dressing gown on.'

'Absolutely not. That's the first step down the slippery slope to senility, in my view. I'll manage, thank you.'

The woman had protested but Martha was adamant. It took her a while, but she managed that night and every other one since. She'd changed the sort of clothes she wore, favouring baggy tee shirts to her normal blouses, and pull-on brightly patterned skirts against the usual sort that did up with a button and a zip. Relieved that it was a hot summer, she'd invested in sandals that did up with Velcro and life was much easier. She was much more comfortable too. Janet had been pleased.

'It was about time you stopped dressing like a teacher,' she said. 'And those clothes take years off you. The others were a bit dated, anyway. Old-fashioned awkward fabrics, too, not easy-care at all. Far too much ironing.'

Martha wondered if she should phone Janet to let her know about the plan, sometimes she rang about half-ten to check Martha was OK. Coming to the conclusion that it would only worry her if nobody answered the phone, she decided to ring her and tell her about Sara's call. Not for the first time, she thought she ought to get herself a mobile phone. It would make life much easier. Perhaps Janet, or Jude, even, might help her get the right one.

'Janet, it's Martha. I'm going to pop over to Jude's house. Sara's coming to collect me in three quarters of an hour, and she's taking me across. Apparently something's come up.'

'Do you want me to come with you?'

'No, there's no need. I'll be absolutely fine. I'll let you know what happens when I see you in the morning, shall I?'

'OK. Good luck, Martha. I hope someone has come up with a solution. See you tomorrow.'

At ten past nine, Sara arrived. She refused to tell Martha what the meeting was about.

'It's quite a complicated story, so I think I can only tell it once, if you don't mind. We'll be there in five minutes. Apparently Micaela should be nearly there by now.'

'Micaela's coming too? All the way from London?'

'Oh yes. This meeting was her idea. She couldn't get away until six—that's why it's had to be so late.'

Jude lived in a mid-terrace red brick house on the outskirts of Gloucester. It took Sara a while to find a parking space. Helping Martha out of the low car, she then opened its back door and took out a bag full of papers.

'She's at number 29. Back this way I think.'

The house opened directly onto the street, and Sara tapped lightly on the emerald green front door. Jude opened it with a broad smile. They could hear the radio playing in a distant room.

'My kids sleep through anything, there's no need to worry about being quiet. Come on in.'

Martha looked round as Jude stepped back to let them in. The living room wasn't big, but it was bright. The walls were painted in a glorious yellow, with flowery curtains and a multicoloured throw over a big battered sofa. A large plastic basket full of toys occupied a corner of the room, and a tower of children's books leant precariously against the wall. Jude had pulled a couple of kitchen chairs into the room to add extra seating.

'Thanks for coming round. Normally I'd ask Mum to babysit, but she's at my sister's house tonight, looking after her kids.'

'Your mother is a big help, isn't she?'

'I couldn't manage without her, to be honest. I don't think any of us could. She keeps threatening that she'll have to retire one day, but I think she's joking. She likes being Grannie Dil too much.' She grinned. 'Well, I hope she's joking, anyway.'

Another knock and Micaela arrived, her usually expressionless face wreathed in smiles.

'Have you told them?'

'Not yet.'

'Told us what? Sit down, please.' Jude could feel the unexpected electricity between Sara and Micaela.

'You start.'

Sara beamed. 'With pleasure. Right, so we all know Graham is a gambler, yes?'

They nodded. 'Well, he hasn't always been a loser. Sometimes he's been very successful, and other people have owed *him* money, instead of the other way round. I don't think he's ever lost such a huge sum before though. Anyway. Matt—from my office, remember?— he and I went through five filing cabinets absolutely full of chaos. Honestly, it was a mess like you've never seen. We found all kinds of things, but the most interesting was this.'

She opened the document case and handed out photocopies of the promissory note they had found on Monday, together with the Google translation.

'It's someone giving Graham a painting in lieu of paying a debt.'

She gave them a moment to read it. 'The only downside is that it doesn't tell us anything about the painting itself.' She took a quick sip of the coffee that Jude had given her, wincing slightly at the quality. The mug had a red flower on it, and the word 'Poppy' in red letters. 'We couldn't find the painting on the walls in my house anywhere, so I thought it must have been sold on. But you know I went to Spain last week, to Calpe to look at Casa Nuevo before it was sold? Well, I bought a little picture from the auction. Before the auction, really, and the assistant was so moody and rude that I made him write out a really full bill of sale for customs, in case I got stopped carrying a piece of hand luggage I hadn't booked in. Then everything kicked off when I got home, and I never unwrapped the thing.'

She looked round at the others, a smile threatening to break out. 'You know what I'm going to say next, don't you? It's too good to be true, almost. We opened the wrapping, and it was the same painting.' She opened her iPad. 'It looks like this.'

'Pretty.'

'It is, isn't it? Not Graham's taste at all, really. That's why I bought it, I think, because it stood out from the rest. Anyway, to cut a long story short—'

'Where is the painting now?'

'I'm coming to that. Yesterday, Matt and I took the picture to the National Gallery, and left it with one of their experts for authentication. And late this afternoon, I got a phone call. It's genuine.'

There was a ripple of astonishment around the room.

'So I contacted Micaela—'

'And I contacted Senor Garcia. He would be willing to take the painting and the money from the Spanish house auction, and the sale of the flat in Greece, as full payment of the debt. Graham could be free by this time on Monday.'

Micaela was ecstatic. Martha looked delighted; Sara and Jude less so.

'So, where will he go?' Sara's voice was level and completely expressionless.

'Graham? He will come back to England of course.'

'I meant, where will he stay?' The tension in Sara's voice was contagious.

Micaela looked at her.

Sara said, 'He's not coming back to my house. I've filed for a divorce. He's not setting a foot in that house.'

Jude said, 'I'd rather he didn't see my kids. It would only confuse them. They know their daddy died in an accident. Anyway, he doesn't like kids. I know that now.'

They looked at Martha.

'I'd love to see him. But I don't know if he wants to see me. I've got used to remembering him aged twenty-seven. In fact, I like to remember him younger, before things went so very wrong. But I'd love to see him again.'

The muscles in Micaela's jaw tightened. "My house." "My kids." Neither of them said "our", she noticed. They had disowned Graham already.

'If you don't want him, he can stay with me, of course. He is my husband too.'

'Well, no, Micaela, he isn't, is he? Not really.'

'Well, he will be, Sara. We will get married as soon as he is divorced.'

'Really? After all his lies?'

'Yes. I love him. I don't like him much sometimes, but I love him anyway.'

Martha patted her hand. 'I couldn't have put it better myself.'

Jude was sitting quite still. 'What I want to know,' she said, 'Is what this will mean to my kids? Keira and Robbie. Their birth certificates are a lie. How do I correct them? And then what? What if they see their birth certificates later and ask about their father; where he is, why he didn't want them? I've always said that he went away. Poppy knows that means he's dead, but the twins are too little to understand. They'll think I lied. What will it do to them?'

'You could always tell them the truth, that he's a lying, self-centred cheating arsehole.'

'Sara.'

'Well.' She shrugged. 'Tell me what I just said isn't true and I'll apologise. I'm sorry if I hurt your feelings, Martha, but I'm not sorry I said it. It's the truth, and he's very, very lucky indeed that we don't just sell the painting and split the money four ways. I'm sure Jude

193

would find that money very helpful, raising three kids without their dad, wouldn't you?'

Jude put her head on one side and pulled a wry face.

'It is what it is,' she said. 'I've never known anything different, I suppose. He wasn't around much after Poppy was born, even. I don't suppose she even remembers his face. I didn't mean to get pregnant again, not that I'd be without the twins, of course I wouldn't, but it's tough, being a single mum.' Martha nodded and looked at her feet. Sara stared glassily at the ceiling, willing herself not to offer to swap with Jude at a moment's notice. She wondered whether it would seem odd if she asked to peek at the sleeping children.

'Sara's friend Matt has offered to be the go-between,' Micaela continued. 'He will meet with Garcia's representative at a lawyer's office of our choosing. The exchange of money and the picture will take place, and Matt will receive a note clearing Graham in full of any and all debts. Garcia will pay for Matt's plane ticket.'

'It's very good of Matt to do this. He won't be in any danger, will he?'

'We don't think so. And yes, it is good of him. He's a decent man.' Sara put a slight stress on the word 'he'.

'There's no risk is there, Micaela?'

'No. It's quite safe, I promise you. To Garcia, honour is all. We have his word. He will not break his word.' She looked at Sara. 'He has suggested that you meet at his head office. It's a good idea, I think. There will be many witnesses.'

At that moment, Micaela's phone rang. She looked at the display and frowned. One word appeared on the screen. *Elena.*

'Si.'

A rapid conversation in Spanish followed, with Micaela becoming more panic-stricken and noisy with each passing moment. She switched the phone off and stood up abruptly. The kitchen chair she was sitting on started to topple, and she grabbed it absent-mindedly, pulling her shoulder bag off the back of the chair and swinging it across her body. She didn't look at them as she tucked her phone inside the bag.

'I have to go.'

'Has something happened? Are you all right?' Jude was on her feet, ready to offer assistance.

'Is my cousin, Elena. She look after Graham. She will not wake him. He sleep too deep. I have to get to him.' Micaela was clearly thinking in Spanish and speaking in tumbled English.

'Is he dead?'

Martha said it very quietly. Jude and Sara both moved to sit next to her. Jude held her good hand.

'No, she don't think so. He will not wake. She gives him some pills to keep him quiet, I think maybe he has had too many. I have to go.'

She was at the door.

'Have they called an ambulance?'

'How can they? He is chained in the cellar. How can they explain that?' As soon as she said the words, Micaela realised she'd given them information she had decided to keep secret. Gritting her teeth, she froze, braced for the backlash.

'Chained?'

'It was not safe for him to be able to get out. He is not always clever. It was safer to chain him.'

'You chained him up? Like a dog? How could you?'

Tears were pouring down Martha's cheeks; her face has lost its pallor and hectic spots of colour were rising on her cheeks in her tense fury.

'Tell them to make him drink milk,' Jude said, 'lots of milk. Pour it in and in. Get him to walk. Tell them to shout at him. Shake him, hard. Get him to a hospital somehow.'

Micaela nodded at Jude's advice and was gone.

Sara put her arm round Martha's shaking shoulders. 'He'll be all right. He'll just sleep it off. He's tough, your Graham. It'll be all right. We'll get him home.'

She wished she felt as certain as she sounded.

If Micaela spotted the black Mercedes that tailed her back to London, she was too distraught to notice it. In that car the two men had cheered up. This was more like it. They'd been stuck in England for over a week with nothing but old women's tea parties to report back on. Micaela Fernandez was clearly in a hurry, something must have happened. They followed her home, and then nipped into the all-night supermarket at the top of her street to get themselves a congratulatory beer and some supplies for the night shift. This, they told each other, was where they could start feeling like real agents. They missed the taxi that took Micaela to Heathrow.

Crime Lord

In the car, Micaela yelled at her hands-free as she negotiated all the endless roundabouts through the outskirts of Gloucester. 'Siri, phone José Garcia.'

'Phoning José Garcia.' The digital voice sounded metallic in the darkness. The phone rang on and on.

Eventually a cross voice answered. 'Si?'

'Senor Garcia, this is Micaela Fernandez. Can we talk?'

Coded speak for, "Are you alone?"

'It's late. You call me tomorrow.' Micaela glanced at the clock—Spain was an hour ahead. It was almost midnight there.

'No. No. Don't hang up. Please, Senor, I need your help.'

A heavy sigh the other end of the line. 'They will not agree to the painting?'

'Yes, they agree, but I have a major problem, it's about Graham Parker.'

'What about him now?' The voice took on a cold note.

'He's desperately ill.'

'Hah.'

'No, really, I'm telling you the truth. He's been drugged, over-sedated. I think he may die.' Her voice cracked.

'Send him to a hospital, then.'

'I can't, I'm in England. The woman who drugged him is too scared to call for help.'

'He is here in Espana?' Garcia's voice rose in surprise. He'd had men tailing Micaela in England, convinced she would lead him to her man.

'Yes. I was hiding him from you there.'

'Sensible woman. But now you want my help?'

'Yes. Please, Senor, please. I'm begging you. Please send someone to get him and take him to a hospital. Please.'

There was silence on the other end of the phone.

'You trust me not to kill him?'

Now it was Micaela's turn to hesitate. This answer was important.

'Not entirely. But I'm asking you as a man of honour.'

A bark of laughter. 'A risky tactic, Senora. Where is he?'

'You'll not hurt him?'

'You have my word.'

'He's in Calpe.' She gave the address.

'But this is right under my nose. This is practically the next road to Casa Nuevo.' He was laughing again. 'Senora, you are either quite mad or very brave. You should maybe change your job, come and work for me.'

'Please, Senor, please send someone right now. I'm on my way as fast as I can, but I won't be there before the morning. I'll tell my cousin Elena you are sending some people, so she won't resist your help.'

'Elena is the woman who drugged this foolish man?'

'Yes. She was only trying to keep him safe, to keep him quiet.'

'Let's hope he isn't quiet forever, eh, Senora

198

Fernandez? I will send now.'

'Thank you. Oh, thank you.' Micaela had stopped trying to hide her emotions. 'He is chained, Senor. Elena can't find the key.'

The laughter grew louder. 'Formidable. A woman with *cojones*. You definitely should consider my offer of employment.' Micaela said nothing, but pushed her foot down harder on the accelerator.

'And, Senora Fernandez.' All the laughter had gone from his voice.

'Si.'

'I will have the painting as arranged, no matter what the outcome. If he dies, the painting is still mine.'

'Si. Gracias, Senor, gracias.'

Sara was torn. The meeting had broken up in chaos, and they had driven back to Martha's big, empty house in silence. There seemed to be nothing anybody could say to comfort Martha, who had retreated into herself, becoming rigid and unapproachable. Sara didn't want to leave Martha like this. The old woman was shaking and pale.

'I'll be fine. You go, you've got a long drive.'

'It's just to Stratford. It's only an hour.'

'That's quite far enough at this time of night. I'll be fine, honestly. Micaela will ring when she has some news. There's nothing we can do now. It's in the lap of the gods.' Her voice was quite flat, and Sara sensed that Martha was keen for her to leave, so that she could finally let go of the tight grip she had over her emotions.

'If you're sure you'll be all right?'

199

'I am. Off you go.'

One-handed, awkwardly, Martha poured herself a large measure of brandy and sat down in the old-fashioned, upright armchair by the window, staring out into the dark. It shouldn't be like this. Mothers shouldn't sit worrying about the death of their children. She sipped the brandy, wrinkling her nose at the taste and feeling the heat of the spirit as it travelled through her. There should be a button you could press to exchange some of your own years, she was seventy-seven, she could offer the last ten years of her life to whatever god there might be, to pass to Graham. He was still young, still only in his fifties. It wasn't right.

She decided not to go to bed, in case she missed the telephone call. Painstakingly carefully, one step at a time, she brought an ancient tartan travel rug down from the airing cupboard in the spare room, being careful not to trip on the fringing, and then she made herself a flask of strong, sweet coffee. Pouring the kettle with her left hand was tricky, but she was determined and managed. As a final thought, she brought the brandy bottle into the living room too. Then, settling herself as comfortably as possible, she put the television on very quietly, and half-watched reruns of "Poirot" for most of the night.

Janet glanced at the front of Martha's house as she walked up the drive, and was surprised to see Martha already sitting in the tapestry armchair by the window. She put her newly-cut key in the lock and called out, 'Well, you're an early bird, aren't you? You must've been

200

up with the lark. Isn't it a beautiful day?' Then she took the whole picture in. Martha looked befuddled and stiff. She was clearly very cross and embarrassed to be caught dozing in an armchair, too.

'Did you spend the whole night here? Were you stuck? Oh Martha.'

'I was NOT stuck at all. I made a conscious decision to remain close to the telephone. I am expecting an important phone call.' Martha was at her haughty best.

'Right. But you could've just plugged the phone in next to your bed, couldn't you? Did you think you might sleep through the ring?'

'Damn. I didn't think of that. I forgot there was a phone point up there. Oh, I'm going senile, I know I am.'

'Don't be silly, of course you're not. You're stressed, and tired and you've not been well.'

'Will you please stop treating me like an invalid. I'm perfectly well, I just had a bit of an accident.' She pushed back the tartan blanket and stood up creakily. 'And if you don't get out of my way right now, I shall have another accident of a different sort. I'll explain in a minute,' she added over her shoulder, making good speed towards the downstairs loo. 'Hang on.'

Amused, but concerned, Janet folded the rug neatly and took the flask and the bone china mug into the kitchen to wash them up. She took the brandy glass too, wondering what had happened to make the almost-teetotal Martha turn to drink. By the level of the bottle, she'd had a couple of stiff ones. She heard the toilet flush and put the bottle back in the cabinet quickly, turning away and running the hot tap to wash up the few supper things as well.

'Have you had any breakfast?'

'No. And I don't want any, either. Just coffee will be fine.'

Janet switched on the kettle and took two cups and saucers from the dresser. She waited till Martha had sat down and then started asking questions.

'Let me drink my coffee, and then I'll tell you. Can we hear the phone from in here?'

'Yes. Well I can, anyway. If it rings, I'll get it.'

'You used to be more polite to me than this.'

'That was before we were friends.'

'Touché.'

'Martha, I've been thinking.'

'Oh Lord.'

'Never mind.'

'Oh, go on. Spit it out.'

At that moment the telephone burst into life.

'Quick. You've got to get that. It'll be Micaela.'

Sensing this was urgent, Janet ran. She snatched up the phone.

'Yes?'

'Martha?

'Janet.'

'Is Micaela. Tell Martha he's in the hospital. I don't know any more yet, but he's in the hospital. OK? Tell her he's safe. I'm just at the airport now; I'm driving directly to him. I have to go.'

The line went dead. Martha was standing by the table, a look of dread on her face. 'Tell me.'

'Micaela says he's safe, he's in the hospital.'

She caught the old lady as her knees gave way under her.

'Martha?'

'I'm fine, I'm fine.' She waved Janet away. 'I just need a minute, that's all.'

Concerned, curious and cross all at the same time, Janet helped her to a chair and took the one opposite. She sat and waited. Martha took several deep breaths to compose herself before she spoke. Her voice was level, but her fingers folded and folded the edge of the tablecloth into tiny pleats while she was talking.

'You know Micaela said she had Graham in a safe place?'

'Yes.'

'Well.' Janet watched Martha take a firm control of whatever emotion was threating to overwhelm her. She swallowed hard and forced her shoulders back. 'Well, the safe place was an earth cellar. A sort of shelter dug at the end of the garden, like a Nissen Hut. Graham was being difficult, it seems, headstrong, noisy. And they were frightened that he would try to get out, and that this thug would send some men to find him and kill him, so they chained him up to stop him leaving.'

'What? Chained him—?'

'Quite. And then they drugged him to keep him quiet, so the neighbours wouldn't hear him.'

'How long has he been in there?'

'Almost three weeks, from what I gather.'

'Oh my God.'

'Yes, my God indeed. And then whoever was

203

supposed to be looking after him managed to give him an overdose. Last night, when we were all at Jude's, Micaela got an hysterical phone call. The woman who was drugging him couldn't wake him. She wouldn't call an ambulance because she couldn't explain his being locked in her cellar, and she couldn't get him out by herself.'

'Jesus.' Martha gave Janet a severe look. 'Sorry, go on.'

'So, I've no idea what Micaela did, but somehow she's managed to get him out of there. Thank God.'

Janet shook her head in disbelief. 'Chained AND drugged?'

'Mmm. And she says she loves him.'

'God. I hope he never makes her really cross. Who knows what she'd do then?' She caught Martha's eye. Despite the awfulness of the situation, Martha felt a bubble of laughter in her chest. 'I know. That's what I kept thinking last night.'

'So is that what the meeting was about?'

'No. No, THAT was good news. That's paled rather in the light of Graham's collapse. Sara has found a painting that Graham was once given in payment for a large debt that he was owed, and it's worth a lot of money. I don't know quite how much, but enough money, anyway. And this Crime Lord, or whatever he is, has agreed to take it as balance for the debt and let Graham go safely. He'll be able to come home.' Her voice tailed off.

'If he survives.'

'Yes. Succinct as ever, Janet. If he survives.'

Good Samaritans

Graham was almost as white as the sheet he was lying on. Well, Micaela admitted to herself more accurately, he was very pale, at least. He was also filthy, and surprisingly thin. The dark circles around his eyes and the beard that had grown since he went into hiding had changed his image completely. His hands were ingrained with dirt and his once beautifully manicured fingernails were torn and blackened. He looked like a tramp, like one of the homeless people who called for spare change from boarded-up shop doorways. Micaela covered her mouth with her hand. He smelled revolting too. Mildew, sweat, vomit and worse. She had been trying to keep him safe.

'Do you know this man?' The doctor, sparkling clean in contrast to the disgusting state of his patient, was clearly intrigued to see this elegant, attractive woman looking so concerned about an old tramp.

'Yes. Well—a little, anyway.'

'What is his name?'

'Graham something. Porter? No, Parker, I think he said.'

'He is not Spanish?'

'No. I believe he's from England.'

'Someone will have to pay to get him home. Does he have insurance?'

'I've no idea. Probably.' Even as she said it, she doubted it. 'Will he live?'

'We will see. He is in a pretty bad way. Has he lived

on the streets long?'

So they thought he'd been brought in as a street-person too.

'Not long, I think. Who brought him in?'

'Some men found him collapsed outside a bodega and I think they called an ambulance.' He checked his notes. 'No, they carried him in themselves.' He wrinkled his nose in distaste. 'I hope they get their car valeted thoroughly. God alone knows what it must smell like now. They were Good Samaritans indeed.'

Garcia's men wouldn't like being called Good Samaritans, Micaela thought. It would amuse Senor Garcia though.

'What is your relationship with Mr Parker, Senora?'

'We're just friends—well, barely even that, really.' She had to be careful. She didn't want to be landed with the hospital bill. 'He has nothing. No money. Nowhere to live. His wife has thrown him out and he has no job.'

The doctor snorted. 'So he has come to Spain to drown his sorrows in the sunshine and scrounge a living from the tourists while he's at it?'

'No, I don't think so. I think his life has just suddenly gone wrong.'

'It happens. Do you want to wait?'

'Yes, I'll wait. Someone should.'

She sat by the bed and stared at this unfamiliar, filthy, cadaverous Graham. She'd wait forever if necessary.

At work, Jude found she couldn't concentrate at all. Her mind kept flicking back to that awful conversation. She heard herself saying, 'I'd rather he didn't see my kids,' again and again. Was that the right thing to do? She was their mother; she needed to protect them—and he—he wasn't a real father. He was barely more than a sperm donor, for all the parenting and love he'd offered. What sort of man fakes his own death to avoid childcare, for Chrissake? He hadn't even had the decency to tell her the truth, which was that he didn't want to know them any more. She'd never had a single penny from him to help her raise them, either.

'Jude? Jude? Earth to Sister Richards?'

'Sorry, I was away in a world of my own then.'

'I'll say. And not a good world, by the look on your face. Kids playing up again?'

She resented the "again". 'No, actually. Just a man.'

'Ooh, a new love interest? You've kept that all to yourself.'

'No such luck. I was just thinking about a rather unpleasant man I used to know.'

Karen was intrigued. 'Tell me, then.'

'No, he's a waste of air.' Her tone became professional. 'What can I help you with, Karen?'

'Mrs Blakeney says she's in pain. Can we do something or does she have to wait?'

Jude read the chart Karen was offering. 'See if she'll settle for a couple of Paracetamol. If she says that won't be enough, page the attending.'

'OK.' Karen took the chart back. 'Sure you don't want to talk about it? A problem shared, and all that?'

'Absolutely, thanks.' She'd chat with Dilys later. The last thing she needed was Karen spreading gossip round the place.

Sara, desperate for any kind of distraction, had gone in to work. They were pleased to see her back and asked how things were going. Mentally, she braced herself. Now was as good a time as any to tell them.

'Well, I've decided to divorce Graham.'

There was a flurry of surprise around the room and a few concerned questions. She caught some glances between her colleagues too.

'It's been brought to my attention that he's been seeing other women, and he's got himself involved in some major financial trouble, too. In fact, if anyone wanted to donate their sweepstake winnings to my legal costs, I'd be very grateful.'

They laughed, as she'd intended them to. The last thing she wanted was fake concern or pity. 'So, I'm dealing with it. End of subject. Now, where have we got to with the latest clients? Anything new I should know about?'

Sara spent the morning catching up with paperwork, signing letters, ringing clients to answer their queries and generally troubleshooting. The place, it seemed, had run like clockwork without her. Through her mind the same thought kept circling. 'They don't need me. I could retire; stay as owner and director, but take a back seat. I could sell the house and move somewhere else, where people didn't know me; I could make a new start.'

Wendy had stuck her head through the back door this morning before Sara made her way to work.

'Did anything happen while we were away? Found

out any more about Graham yet?'

Sara had promised to fill her in this evening. She hadn't even been aware that Wendy and Brian had been away for almost a week. She thought it had been quiet next door, but she'd been so busy with trying to sort out all the paperwork that she'd barely looked outside. And anyway, she'd kind of taken it for granted that Wendy was sulking after the Pershore meeting, and that was why she hadn't been round. She sighed. Did she really want Wendy to know all this? She could be a good friend, but she loved to gossip, especially after a few glasses of wine. Maybe she could give her a revised version. Leave out a few of the juicier details. She wouldn't tell her that Matt had been staying, for a start. Wendy would immediately presume that they were sleeping together—after all, it's what would happen in the soaps that she was so fond of.

'Knock, knock?'

'Who's there?' Her reply was automatic.

'Typical. I give up the best part of a week sorting out your problems and you can't even remember my name.'

'Matt. Come in.' She was pleased to see him. 'How's it going?'

'Good, thanks. I was going to ask you the same thing. Did they agree about the painting yesterday? Am I still taking it over to Spain?'

The Sorolla painting. In all last night's turmoil she'd stopped thinking about that. It was almost if by agreeing to give it to Garcia, she'd forgotten that it even existed. Easy come, easy go.

'Life got a bit exciting at the meeting, actually.'

'More exciting? My God, Sara, I lead such a simple life.'

'Much more. And no, not exciting, really. That's the wrong word. Horrifying, really. Devastating—for poor Martha, anyway.' She looked at the clock. 'It's practically lunchtime. We can't talk here. Shall we go and get a sandwich at the pub?'

'There'll be talk if we go together.'

'Do you care?'

'No, actually, I don't.' He looked at her. 'Do you?'

She knew what he was saying. A small, secret smile almost crossed her lips. 'Not in the slightest.'

Heads turned as they walked out together.

In the pub, they chose a discreet corner table, and Sara checked the reception on her phone.

'Waiting for news?'

'Yes. Graham's in hospital. He's been taken ill.'

'Stress-related? Has he had a heart attack?'

'Nothing as natural as that. Micaela tried to kill him with kindness.'

'Sorry?'

Sara explained about the late-night phone call.

'Chained *and* drugged?'

'Yup.'

'Blimey. She wasn't taking any risks, was she? Just how dangerous is this Garcia bloke?'

'My guess is that he's not a nice man at all.'

'Wow.' He sipped his pint.

'Look, if you want to pull out of next week's meeting in the light of all this, that's perfectly OK. We'll pay for a courier or something.'

'No, no, I said I'd do it and I will. Will he survive? Graham?'

'I don't know. Micaela said she'd got someone to take him to the hospital, but I've got no idea how. She's a resourceful woman.'

'And not one to be crossed, it seems. Drugged AND chained. My God.' He gave Sara a wicked look. 'Mind you, who are we to judge? Whatever floats your boat, I say.' There was the merest suggestion of a wink and he picked up his sandwich. 'Will you come with me?' His voice was casual, but he didn't meet her eyes.

'Sorry?' Sara was distracted, squinting at her phone in the bright sunlight that lit their table.

'To Spain. Will you come with me?' Sara lifted her head from the screen, astonished. His gaze was steady. 'We could have a few days by the sea, after. Or we could go to Barcelona. I love Barcelona. Have you been?'

'Yes. No. I mean, yes I've been to Barcelona. I'm confused here. What are you asking?'

'Should I maybe have put my request in a memo?'

She narrowed her eyes.

'I was wondering, Ms Parker, are you going to stay a Parker, by the way? I was wondering if you fancied a bit of a holiday. In Spain. With me. Or anywhere else, really. But with me.'

'I—er—I…'

'It's easy, really. You say, "Yes, please, that'd be fun." or "No, thanks, I've always thought you were a bit dull." See? Simple.'

'Well, it isn't really that simple, is it?' She paused. 'Is

211

it?'

'Isn't it? Why not? You're getting divorced, we like each other; it's an opportunity to get to know each other away from all this.' He waved his hands in an all-encompassing fashion, endangering both his pint and Sara's sandwich.

'Together, together?' She caught his glass before it toppled, and bundled her screwed-up paper napkin under her plate to mop up the slopped beer.

'You want separate rooms? We can have separate rooms. But we could have fun, too. Hand over the picture, get the affidavit, shove Graham on a plane if he's up to it, and then drive off into the sunset.'

'You've got it all worked out, haven't you?'

'Yes.' He grinned at her. 'What do you say?'

New Starts

Janet had finished cleaning. She put the dusters in the washing machine and straightened up. Putting both hands on the table and tapping her fingers in a distracted way, she spoke tentatively. 'Martha, about that idea I mentioned before the phone rang and we got distracted.'

'Mmm?'

'My lease is coming up for renewal.'

Janet lived in a flat on the far side of the main road. She'd moved, 'to make a new start' after her husband died, but she'd never really settled into the place. The traffic noise and fumes and the anonymity of living in a flat didn't suit her after years of living in a friendly terraced house with a little garden of her own. In fact, she wasn't even certain what the woman who lived in the flat opposite her was called—and she'd lived there the best part of three years. Janet said hello, if they met, but the woman never seemed like she wanted to strike up a conversation. The truth of the matter was that she didn't suit living alone. She hated having nobody to chat to at home, nobody to make a second cup of tea for. In short, she was lonely. 'What would you think about me moving in here with you?'

Martha looked up sharply.

'I'd pay rent, of course. It just seems daft, me living over there on my own and you living over here in this big house, all alone too. You don't want to move into one of those retirement places, and you're not getting any younger—well, nor am I—we'd be company for each other and I could look out for you, drive you about, cook, clean, that sort of thing?'

'A housekeeper?'

'If you like.'

'But if you paid me rent, and I paid you wages, they'd cancel each other out, really, wouldn't they?'

'Maybe. More or less.' Janet held her breath. She didn't want to seem too desperate, too needy. She had to give Martha space to think this over. It would be a major change for both of them. Martha was a very private person, Janet knew.

'When do you need to know?'

'I've got a month before I have to make my decision on keeping the flat or not.'

'I'll need to think about it. Leave it with me.'

Graham's eyelids fluttered and he sighed. Micaela, alert to every tiny movement, was on her feet in an instant.

'Graham? Graham?'

He swallowed, his eyes still closed. 'Drink?' His voice was thick, and white salty crusts had formed at the corners of his mouth.

Micaela called for a nurse.

'I think he's coming round. He's asking for a drink? Can I give him some water?'

The nurse checked the beeping machine behind the bed, reading the stats that meant nothing to Micaela.

'Little sips, only. I'll get you a straw, it'll be easier. Does he speak Spanish?'

'Si.' The voice from the bed was weak and croaky,

but it was there. 'Yo hablo español.'

The nurse looked immensely relieved. She spoke some English, but everything was so much quicker in Spanish. She nodded at Micaela.

'Just little sips, OK?'

When they walked back into the office, Sara could practically hear the 'rhubarb, rhubarb, rhubarb' of people pretending to be busy. Already, they'd leapt to conclusions, and right at this moment, Sara wasn't sure whether they were right or wrong. Give me a break, she thought. Look at them. Wendy will be just the same. She smiled warmly round the outer office, devilment making her stir up the atmosphere a little more, then went into her own room and closed the door, cruelly leaving Matt to their tender mercies. Picking up her phone, she called Micaela's number. The international dialling tone always confused her with its single beep, too like the UK engaged signal. After a minute, Micaela answered.

'He waked. Just for minute only, but he speaking.'

'You're excited. He'll be OK?'

'Si, Si. Too early to be certain, but they think yes. That's so great, yes?'

'Great.' Sara tried to keep the irony out of her tone. 'How on earth did you get him to hospital? Didn't the ambulance people make a fuss? What about the chains? Did the police come?'

Micaela paused before answering and her tone was slightly defensive. 'I called Senor Garcia and asked for his help.'

'You did what?'

'I asked him, as a man of honour, to help us. It means a lot in Spain, honour.'

'And he helped you?'

'He sent two of his men, with bolt-cutters, to my cousin Elena. She passed out with terror and shock. They took him and left him at the hospital door. Here, they think he is a beggar, a street person. He looks terrible, Sara.'

'But Senor Garcia? You took a hell of a risk, calling him, surely?'

'I couldn't think of another. He is powerful, yes. I couldn't risk that Graham would be dead before I got here. It was very close, I think.'

'And Elena?'

'Elena is fine. She is ashamed she gave him too many pills; she is embarrassed she fainted. She is pleased he is gone; she is cross about the state of her cellar. She will be fine.'

'That seems to cover all the bases.' Sara was amused by Micaela's dismissive tone. 'Do you think Graham will be in hospital for long?'

It felt strange, discussing her husband in this removed way, with a woman who clearly loved him far more than she did, maybe more than she ever had, Sara realised with shock.

'I don't know the answer to this. I will get him out as soon as I can. But he has lost much weight. He looks so ill, so yellow. And the beard will have to go. Ugh.'

'Good luck, Micaela.' Sara meant it. In that moment she made up her mind. 'I'm going to fly over to Spain on Monday with Matt, when he brings the painting. Just to make sure everything goes through properly.'

'Of course.' If she thought anything other than that, Micaela's tone didn't give anything away. 'Will you come here, to the hospital, to see Graham?'

'Oh, I expect he'll have been released by then. And even if he hasn't been, no, I don't think so, Micaela. I have nothing to say to that man. He's all yours. As I said before, I wish you the very best of luck.' As she said it, Sara was thinking, 'You're probably going to need it.'

Spain

Sara put the phone down, her mind a whirl of conflicting emotions. She felt relief, probably, that Graham was likely to get better. Certainly, she was relieved that he hadn't died, chained up like an animal in a stinking cellar, that was for definite. She had no idea how any of them would have handled that one. There was a top note of sadness, too, of what they'd never manage to achieve together; that she hadn't been enough for Graham—but then again, neither had Micaela, after all, look at the way he'd treated Jude. She wondered once again if there were even more women that she didn't know about; ones who'd had the perspicacity to see Graham for what he was, beneath the easy charm; a liar and a rat. They were the lucky ones that got away.

Decisively, she sent Matt a text. 'I think Barcelona would be just great. Will you book a room or shall I?'

His reply was almost instantaneous. 'You choose, I'll pay.'

Sara straightened her back in the chair. This time, life would be different. This time, everything would be out in the open, on equal footing. Her fingers flashed across the keyboard. 'We go halves, or not at all.'

He sent back a GIF. A blue genie, bowing its way out of a magic lantern, 'Your wish is my command.'

Laughing, she pulled the laptop towards her and tapped in a single word. Barcelona.

While Micaela had been standing outside, talking on the phone to Sara, things had suddenly taken a turn for the worse at the hospital. Graham had developed a raging fever, and a hectic flush was staining his lined grey cheeks. He was thrashing about, one minute pushing off the covers, the next, shivering with cold. He kept batting at the drip they'd inserted into the back of his hand, and he was rambling incoherently. Micaela caught the word 'shackled' and hoped that her grasp of English was better than anyone else's in the room.

'We need to get fluids into him, as well as the antibiotics,' the doctor told Micaela. 'He has an infection. It started in his ankle, here, look.'

Graham's ankle was fiery and suppurating where the rusty chains had bitten into his flesh. 'It looks as if he has been kept captive somewhere.'

He looked hard at Micaela. 'How did you say you knew him?'

Micaela thought fast. She'd been half-expecting this, so she had the bones of her story prepared.

'He was begging in a doorway. Begging in three languages. I got talking to him. He wasn't just an ordinary tramp. I saw him in the same doorway three days in a row, so I bought him some sandwiches, and then he wasn't there the next day. Someone said they thought he was here. I came to see if he was all right.'

'You seem pretty concerned for someone you don't know that well.' He eyed her sharply.

Michaela let out a ragged breath. 'He's clearly an intelligent man, and he's had bad luck. It could happen to any of us. He told me about his life. He reminded me of my father.' She was prepared to cry if she had to. She couldn't let the doctor suspect she knew anything about Graham's past, especially not his immediate past.

'Fair enough.' Brusque, to quash her threatening tears, he consulted the chart. 'The next few hours are pretty critical, however. We are watching for gangrene. Are you staying with him? Do you know if he has a next-of-kin? Anybody we should call?'

'I don't know, I'm sorry. I have to make a few phone calls myself, for work, you know how it is? But if it is important, I can stay with him, of course, yes.'

'If you notice any changes, you must let us know. If the room smells different, let us know. If he goes quiet—'

'Let you know. Yes, I've got it.' She paused. 'And if it is gangrene?'

'We may have to amputate his foot; maybe the lower part of his leg.'

'Oh my God—the poor man. How will he cope?'

'We just have to wait and see.'

Grannies-in-law and Guilt

Dilys knocked at Martha's door. 'Yes?' Initially, her mind elsewhere, she didn't recognise the elderly woman standing on her doorstep, and her tone was sharp. 'Oh, Dilys, it's you. I'm sorry—please, come in—I was just in the kitchen. Come and have a cup of tea. I could do with some company.'

'I'm sorry to drop in on you unannounced like this, but I was wonderin' what was going on. Jude was very distracted when she dropped the kids off this morning and we couldn't talk, she was all of a rush. Deliberately, I think.' She peered more closely at Martha. 'You look tired, all this must be taking its toll on you too.'

Martha smiled wearily. 'I didn't get a lot of sleep last night. We had good news and bad news. Would you like a drink?' She clicked the kettle on without waiting for an answer. 'Janet always leaves the kettle filled for me, but you'll have to pour it, I'm afraid. This damn wrist—' She waved her plastered arm.

'Sure. No problem. What news was that then??'

Martha sat down with a sigh. 'Well, the good news is that they've raised the money, they think. The mob boss has agreed to take a painting of Sara's that's worth a small fortune. He'll consider the debt paid.'

'Well, thank the good Lord for that.'

'But now Graham has been rushed to a hospital in Spain. It's touch and go, I think.'

'Has he had a heart attack? Is it all the stress? All the good livin' caught up with him at last?'

'No, none of those. It was an overdose.'

Dilys was shocked. 'He tried to kill himself?' Unconsciously, she crossed herself.

'No. No, where he was in hiding, he wouldn't keep quiet; they were really worried that word would get back to Garcia. And so whoever was hiding him drugged him, you know, with sleeping pills, to calm him down a bit. They were frightened that someone would come to investigate the shouting and banging, and find him. Only it seems they gave him pills with every meal, and then they couldn't wake him up.'

'Oh, dear Lord.' Dilys had her hand over her heart. 'Did they take him to the hospital and explain?'

'No that's where…' Martha had to pause, to get a grip of herself, '…that's where it gets truly dreadful, Dilys. They had him chained up in a cellar. They couldn't get him out, and they couldn't let anybody in to find him like that. They couldn't explain it away.' Her voice was ragged with tears. 'I know he's done dreadful things, Dilys. I know he's wrecked lives. But he's my son—' Her voice failed and she broke down. 'I feel so USELESS. It's my fault, it has to be my fault. I indulged him as a child. It was just him and me, and we only had each other, before Bernard.'

Dilys put a steaming cup of tea on the table in front of Martha and rubbed her arm briskly. 'Come on, come on, you know that's not true. I'm sure you were a great mother. We do the best we can for our kids, all of us.' She handed Martha a piece of kitchen towel. 'Here, have a good blow.'

Martha took the paper gratefully and trumpeted into

it, dabbing at her eyes. 'I've cried more in the last week than for the last two decades. I'm just so worried. They chained him up, Dilys. Like an animal.'

'Terrible. That's just terrible.' Dilys shook her head. 'But he's in the hospital now, you say. How?'

'I don't actually know. Micaela got a flight as soon as she heard. She rang me first thing to say he had been admitted and I've heard nothing since. Now we just wait. I daren't do anything, or go anywhere. I've barely even been to the bathroom, in case I miss the phone. I just feel powerless.' She looked at Dilys. 'It's not right, is it? Any of this. How on earth did any of it happen?'

'No point looking for the whys and wherefores now,' said Dilys, unconsciously echoing her daughter's words. 'It is what it is. It's where we take it from here that matters. Shall I stay with you for a while? We could get to know each other, we're practically related now, aren't we? Grannies-in-law or something?'

'She's lovely, your daughter.' Martha smile was a bit watery. 'A good nurse, too.'

'You'd know, of course. How IS your wrist?'

'It's a bloody nuisance, just between you and me.' They grinned at each other, both of them relieved to change the subject and talk about ordinary matters. 'So, tell me about our grandchildren.'

Dilys rubbed her hands together, and opened her voluminous handbag. 'Well, I thought as you'd missed out a bit, we'd start with some baby photos…'

Micaela didn't know what to do. Every other minute, she was on her feet, checking Graham's forehead, his scarlet ankle, and his pulse. It was still so fluttery and rapid. Suppose they cut his leg off? How would he cope? He'd hate her. At the back of her mind, a small insistent voice kept saying, 'This is your fault. It's all your fault. YOU said to chain him up. YOU said to give him some sleeping pills. You weren't there. You should've been there. This wouldn't have happened if it wasn't for you.' The words went round and round in her head. 'Esto es tu culpa, tu culpa…Your fault, your fault, your fault.'

'I was trying to help,' she protested silently. 'I was trying to raise the money, to save his life, I love him.'

'Funny way of showing it,' the little voice continued insistently, 'and if they DO amputate his foot, he'll tell, you know. He'll tell them that you did this. He won't take any responsibility for getting you into this mess at all, you know he won't. You'll go to jail for kidnapping him. You and Elena too. D'you reckon he'll love you after that? D'you reckon he loves you now?'

'Shut up. Shut up.'

'Mic?' The voice from the bed was weak but lucid. 'I feel like shit.'

'I know you do, baby, I know.' She stroked his forehead. 'They're helping you. You've got a drip. Don't.' She stayed his hand as he scratched at his cannula. 'They're giving you antibiotics, you've got a needle in there. You've picked up an infection somewhere.'

'Garcia?'

'Garcia's happy. I've sorted Garcia.'

His eyelids fluttered. 'I knew you would. I knew you

would help me. Mic.'

He trailed off, back into sleep, or unconsciousness, she couldn't tell which.

Latest News

'Any news?' Matt stuck his head round Sara's office door.

'No, not yet. I was just thinking that perhaps I ought to ring Micaela again?'

'I'm sure she'll ring you if there's any news. I wouldn't worry. He's in the right place now.' He lowered his voice. 'Any more thoughts on Barcelona? Have you looked at hotels?'

Feeling slightly self-conscious, Sara nodded. 'Come in, look at this.' She turned her laptop round.

Jude wondered if there was any way she could hack into the Spanish hospital computer system, or maybe even legitimately contact the team that was nursing Graham there. She didn't speak enough Spanish for a proper discussion, but she'd looked up the words for "alive" and "dead", that was a start. She looked at the clock again. Her shift ended in an hour. She could wait and call Micaela then. She wondered how much ringing a Spanish mobile would cost, and whether she had enough credit left on her phone, even. It was all bloody Graham Parker's fault that she was always broke. If she hadn't met him, she could have had a normal life by now, with a partner to share her life with, and maybe even a planned baby. She brushed the thought aside angrily. She could cope, couldn't she? She didn't need anybody. Nobody would take her on with three kids, anyway, she'd have to cope. Bloody man.

At five-thirty, Wendy bustled into Sara's kitchen, eyes sparkling, avid for information. 'So, what's been happening since you went to meet those women? Have you managed to catch up with Graham? What did he say?'

Sara deflected the questions with one of her own. 'Have you been away? The place has been quiet without you. I'm sure that poor cat's gone into a decline.' She opened the fridge door and took out a bottle of Pinot gris, then busied herself finding glasses, eventually settling for two clean ones from the top of the dishwasher. They were still slightly warm, but she ignored that, chucking an ice cube in each glass, and spinning it round a few times before tipping it down the sink. She needed to buy herself some thinking time.

'Oh, not really away. Brian's mother was taken ill again, so we went up to Grantham to see her. She gave us quite a scare, I can tell you, but she's all right now. We're thinking we'll put her in a home, can't be flying up and down the A46 like a yoyo all the time.'

Sara thought she sounded as if she was talking about a piece of rather awkward furniture that needed to be put in storage.

'What, a care home in Grantham, you mean?'

'Oh no, one here in Stratford. There's a big one just opened up at Binton. That's only a couple of miles.'

'But she won't know anybody there.'

'She knows us. She'll make more friends. They probably do group stuff—chairobics and all that. She'll be fine. Let's face it, with luck it won't be for that long anyway.' Wendy dismissed her mother-in-law callously. 'So, what about you?'

Sara considered her reply carefully before she answered. Wendy was enjoying all this intrigue, she could tell. Sara's pulse quickened in her throat, and she felt resentful of being "entertainment". She poured the wine, only filling the glasses half-way. She didn't want to encourage Wendy to stay for too long.

'Well, he wasn't at the auction, as you know. It turns out he was in hiding, in fact. He'd got into debt, a bit, to the wrong sort of people.'

'Loan sharks?' Wendy took the proffered wine. This week's nails were pale blue, painted with little sailing ships.

'Something like that, yes. In Spain.'

Wendy nodded as if she knew everything there was to know about Spanish loan sharks.

'So that was why he was selling the holiday house?'

'Yes, that's right.'

'And has he paid them off?'

'Yes, he's out of debt now.'

'Well, that's good, isn't it? I bet you're relieved. And what about that wedding picture? With that dark woman? Did you find out about that? Who is she?'

'Just some girl he conned, years ago. In fact, Wendy, I may as well tell you now, I've decided to divorce Graham.'

'Divorce him?'

'Yes.'

'Oh. Right. Good for you.' Wendy sipped her wine thoughtfully, and looked at the floor. She didn't seem as surprised by this as Sara had thought she might be. 'I don't know whether I should say this.'

'But you're going to.'

'Yes. He made a pass at me, once. Well, more than once, really. I just laughed it off. Thought he'd had too much to drink. But maybe—'

'Maybe he was trying his luck?'

'Yes. I told him to get lost, honest I did, Sara. We're friends. I wouldn't do that to you. And besides, Brian would've killed him.' She drained her glass, tipping it a little higher than necessary to let Sara know that she'd noticed the half-measures.

Sara sat back and poured them both another half-glass of wine.

'The thing is, Wendy, I don't really care any more. I think I always knew he was a flirt. I couldn't really expect him to work away all that time and live like a monk.'

'But *you* did. Live like a nun, I mean, not a monk. I suppose I mean, that.' She chuckled at the thought. 'Isn't this where we do a series of "bad habit" nun jokes?'

'Let's not, eh?'

'No. Sorry.'

They drank in silence for a while, and then Wendy said, 'What will you do?' Her blue nails tapped lightly on the bowl of the wineglass, indicating the rapidly falling level of its contents. Sara ignored the prompt.

'How do you mean?'

'Will he come back here? Will you move? Who gets the house? Will I lose you as my neighbour?'

'Oh God, I haven't thought that far ahead yet. He's not coming back here while I've got breath in my body, that's for certain. He's still seeing Micaela in fact.'

'Micaela?' Sara could see Wendy wracking her brains.

'The other bride.'

'Ah, yes, the tarty one in the spray-on frock. I knew she was called something odd. He's still with her? You mean he's been with you both all these years?' There was a gleam in Wendy's eyes.

'Yes.' Sara knew at that moment she was NEVER going to tell Wendy about Jude and her kids.

'The bastard.'

'Yes, well, he can marry her properly now. I wash my hands of him. In fact, I'm—'

She stopped herself in time. She wouldn't tell Wendy about Matt, either. Not yet anyway. At least she hadn't been at home to see him at Sara's house for days on end. Sara decided to wait and see how that turned out first.

'In fact you're what?'

'I'm reminded of what that man said about marrying your mistress.'

'I don't know that one?'

'Apparently it's a mistake to marry your mistress, because it leaves a position vacant.'

Wendy roared with laughter. 'Well, good riddance to them both. I'm glad you seem sorted, Sara. I was worried for you.' She drained her glass. 'I better go. Brian'll be wanting his tea.'

And an update, thought Sara. But she smiled and refused another invitation to join them for supper.

Brian had been coerced into making his famous spagbog yet again. Sara had eaten it once. That was enough.

'I've got lots of things to sort out here, thanks Wend.'

Wendy nodded understandingly and waved as she went back past the kitchen window. For a brief moment, Sara considered putting a bolt on her side of the gate.

'Brian, you'll never guess what's happened now, Sara and Graham are getting a divorce, just like I said before. Remember that other wedding picture I told you about? Brian, are you listening to me? Brian?'

Dilys had left at three o'clock to pick up Jude's children from school. Martha would have liked to go with her, but she still hadn't heard from Micaela, so she didn't want to leave her house. She didn't dare use the phone, either, in case Micaela was trying to call. She sat and fretted. Daytime TV was such a load of old rubbish. She flicked through the channels, trying to find something that wasn't antiques or ghost hunting. "Countdown" would do. She was trying to work out the maths puzzle when the phone rang, and she jumped, even though she was expecting it to ring. The line was crackly, and Martha strained to listen.

'Martha?'

'Yes. Micaela?'

'Si. How are you?'

'Never mind me, how is Graham?'

'He is really not well, Martha. He has an infection in

his blood. Septicaemia, they say. He is on very strong drugs indeed.'

'Oh God.' Martha paused, steeling herself to ask the question. Her mouth was dry, and she had to swallow before she spoke again. 'Will he die?' She'd never said it out loud before. She wondered whether she was calling up devils by giving voice to her dread.

'They are still not sure.' She hesitated. 'They say that he might have to have an operation, Martha.'

'An operation? What for?'

There was a silence. Martha waited. She could imagine Micaela struggling to compose herself. 'They may have to amputate his foot.' Her voice was quiet, and Martha wondered for a moment if she'd misheard. 'His foot?'

'Si. Yes. He has an infection. From the dirty place he was living.'

'Your cousin's cellar, you mean?' Martha's voice was accusatory.

'Shhh. I cannot let them know this. To them, he is a street person. A down and out.'

Martha closed her eyes. She had to keep a grip on herself. Keeping her voice level, she asked 'Do you need anything? Money? Will you tell me if they decide to do it?'

'Yes. No, I don't need anything. I'm so sorry, Martha. I was trying to keep him safe. Honestly I was. I never imagined that this would happen. You must believe me.' Her voice was full of tears.

Martha struggled to keep control. 'I know. You were only doing what you thought was best. Please, keep me informed. You promise? No matter what it is, no matter how bad, I need to know.' Micaela rang off, leaving Martha holding on to a strange foreign dialling tone. On the TV, Susie Dent was explaining the meaning of the phrase 'left high and dry'. It seemed strangely appropriate, somehow.

Sara couldn't believe it when Micaela rang her with the news.

'Cut off his foot?'

'Because of gangrene. They are worried about gangrene.'

'Christ Almighty. Where did you keep him, in a pit?'

Sara had imagined the cellar to be like the one in the house her parents had owned, with a waxed pine doorway and stone stairs down from the kitchen; a room full of neat racks of jars and bottles, half a broken lawnmower, (sacrificed annually for its parts to keep the other mower in the shed alive), some camping equipment and other general household detritus. She'd had a den in there herself as a girl, and she and her friends used to tell each other ghost stories by torchlight, until they'd either scared themselves silly or grown out of it, she couldn't remember which.

'It was an earth cellar, at the end of the garden. Most Spanish houses have them—for vegetables, you know? It was dry.'

'Sounds like that was all it had going for it. When will they do it?'

'Tomorrow, maybe. They may not have to.'

'Because he'll be better, or because he'll be dead?'

She hadn't meant to sound so brutal. Micaela's voice was very quiet indeed.

'One of those things, yes, Sara. One of those two things.'

Sara was overwhelmed with guilt when she heard the pain in the other woman's voice. She just wanted to wake up tomorrow and find she'd dreamt the whole thing. Maybe as far back as meeting Graham in the first place. 'I'm sure he'll be OK, Micaela. He's in the best place.' It was what you said, wasn't it?

Do You Trust Me?

When Jude came to pick the children up from Dilys after her shift, her nerves were taut. Dilys took one look at her youngest daughter and sat her firmly in a kitchen chair, ushering the kids into the other room with a packet of crisps each and a DVD of *Frozen*, a rare treat. She closed the door.

'What's the matter now?'

Jude shook her head. 'Nothing. I'm fine. It was just a long day, that's all.'

'I know about Graham being in hospital, Judith.'

'You do? How?'

'I went to see Martha, of course. The poor woman's in a terrible state. That bloody man.'

'Mum!' Dilys NEVER swore.

'Well, I'm sorry, Jude, but he makes my blood boil, he really does. Look at you—all of you—Martha and Sara and Micaela and you and the kids. All in complete uproar because one man can't behave himself decently. If I got my hands on him now—' Her face was fierce as she turned away.

'Micaela rang me. He's got septicaemia, Mum. They're watching for gangrene. He might lose his foot.'

'Shame.'

'Mum.'

'Don't you "Mum" me, Judith Richards. I wish you'd never set eyes on him. He'll get what he deserves. "What goes around comes around," isn't that what they say?'

'He might not live, Mum.'

'So? You thought he was dead anyway. Don't waste your tears on him, girl. Save them for his mother.'

'Oh, God, poor Martha, you're right. I should go and see her, I should check she's all right.'

'I rang that Janet. She's a sound, sensible woman. She's going to pack a few things in a bag and go and stay with her for a few days. I think she and Martha have been thinking along the lines of her moving in, anyway. This might decide it, one way or the other. Martha shouldn't be alone, not with this hanging over her like the sword of Damocles.' She looked at Jude. 'You look completely wiped out. Have you eaten anything today?'

'Oh, the usual. You know how it is. A bite here, a swig of cold tea there.'

'Right.' Dilys marched across the kitchen and opened the fridge door. 'It'll have to be pasta.'

The fever broke at midnight. Micaela, dozing in an uncomfortable plastic armchair by the side of the hospital bed, had woken to the sound of total silence. Graham was completely still. She stared at him, alarmed, terrified, but trying to see if he was still breathing, frightened to even move to confirm whether he was dead or alive. She crept to the door on bare feet. A nurse looked up from the screen in front of her a questioning look on her face.

'Could you, uh, could you come and see?'

Sensing Micaela's panic, the nurse got swiftly to her feet and nipped past her into the cubicle. She checked the machines, feeling Graham's neck for a pulse at the same time. Looking at Micaela, she gave one assertive nod.

'The antibiotics are working. He's asleep now. You should try and get some sleep as well.'

'His foot? What about his foot?'

'We'll see. I'll check every couple of hours. There's no real change yet.'

Micaela hadn't been aware she was holding her breath until she let it out.

'OK.'

'Get some rest.'

Sara was in their bedroom, tears she was unaware of streaming down her face as she furiously packed all Graham's things into a second big suitcase. One wardrobe was empty already, and she'd started on the chest of drawers. For a man who lived here on average for three months of the year, he had so much stuff. His shoes alone filled an entire holdall. He'd bought so many toiletries and grooming products, as well, half of them well beyond their "use before" dates. Fetching a black plastic bag, she began to dump the bottles and jars, moving faster and faster as she did it. The final shelf in the bathroom cabinet just got swept in with one vast swoosh of her hand, a bottle of aftershave breaking as it hit the top of the toilet cistern on its way to the bin. The room filled with the familiar smell of Hugo Boss and Sara stood stock still, remembering.

What if he died?

The last couple of weeks had turned her world

upside down. Nothing seemed real any more, she couldn't focus; she had no anchor. Perhaps she was packing the wrong stuff. Perhaps she should pack her own things, everything that meant something to her, and then just walk away and leave the rest. Just torch the place.

She shook her head, trying to rattle some order into it. She sighed, pulled herself up tall and went downstairs to fetch a newspaper to wrap up the broken glass. Opening a window wide to let the fumes of aftershave out, she gave herself a stiff talking to:

'My marriage has always been unusual, to say the least. Graham has always been a philanderer. I'm lucky to escape this whole debacle with a roof over my head. I'm only fifty. That's young. Matt wants to take me to Barcelona.' A small smile sneaked in, despite her best intentions. 'I AM packing the wrong things. I should be packing for a few days away with a new man, not tidying up after the old one.'

Defiantly, she squirted air-freshener on top of the aftershave. The resulting fumes made her back out of the bathroom, coughing. The small voice in her head dropped one last toxic thought in. 'But what if Graham dies, Sara? Will you be able to live with that?' She closed the bathroom door firmly, and answered the little voice out loud. 'Yes.'

Graham was dreaming. He was sitting in a vast room, bedecked with crystal chandeliers and dancing with candlelight. It was noisy in the room, although he couldn't make out any of the conversations that were going on. He knew that he was sitting at the head of a huge dining table, which was populated with women as far as the eye could see. They were all ignoring him, chattering amongst themselves. He tried to catch their attention, but nobody would look his way, no matter what he said or did. He tried to climb on the table so they would see him, but one of his feet was three times the size it should have been, and growing larger and larger as he stared at it, horrified. It was inflating like a balloon in front of his eyes. It throbbed redly, in time with the music around him, as though it was in a cartoon, and he was certain it would explode. He tried to yell for help, but nobody could hear him. He was getting desperate.

Frantically he searched the women's faces, and started to recognise people he knew. Sara was there. She stood up and walked towards him, saying nothing. Her face was completely emotionless, as though she was wearing a mask. Another woman, further down the table, got to her feet. She was tall and elegant. He struggled for her name. Judith? Jude, that was it. She stood silently next to Sara, waiting. He tried to speak to them, to explain, but no words would come out. They stared at him, unnerving him, then turned beckoned to another woman, older, walking more hesitantly.

Oh God, it was his mother. But when had she got so old? She wouldn't look at him, keeping her chin high and her eyes averted when he tried to explain. Explain what? His foot was pulsing angrily now. There were other faces that he recognised in the crowds. Barmaids, temporary secretaries, club hostesses, shop assistants, receptionists. Women of no consequence.

Finally Micaela stood up. She spoke to all the women, although he couldn't hear what she was saying. The noise in the room died down. She turned to him.

'I can make them all go away, Graham,' she said. 'I can make all this disappear. If you trust me, I can make all this better. Do you trust me, Graham?'

And he suddenly found that he did. Micaela would sort it out. Why had he ever doubted her? 'Micaela?'

She was on her feet in an instant, holding his hand by the side of the bed.

'Graham? Graham, you're in hospital. You've been ill, really ill, but you're going to be all right. You're going to get better, Graham. Trust me, you're going to get better.'

Her words echoing his confused dream calmed him, somehow. 'Marry me?'

The tears coursed down her face, at odds with her teasing tone. 'What, again?'

'I'll get a divorce. Sara will understand. We'll explain. We'll do it properly this time.'

She stroked the greying hair back from his face.

'We'll talk about it when you're better.'

Alive?

Janet took the phone call. Martha was dozing in the chair, still refusing to go to bed.

'His fever broke. He's over the worst, now. He's going to live.'

Janet breathed out slowly.

'And his foot? Will he keep his foot?'

'It'll be OK. There'll be some scarring, and they've removed his smallest toe, but it'll be OK. They're talking about discharging him already.'

'Surely not?'

'I'll get him back to the UK, somehow. We'll see what the doctors there think.'

'Is he well enough to fly? What about DVT and things like that?'

'I'll get advice. Will you tell Martha?'

'Yes, I'll tell her.'

'OK. Thanks. I'll ring the others.'

She rang off. Janet was aware that Martha was awake and watching her, her face frozen and still.

'You'll tell me what?'

'He's going to be OK. He won't lose his foot.'

'He's going to live?'

'Oh yes.' Janet's face was unreadable. 'He's going to live.'

It was Monday morning. Matt, Sara and the Sorolla painting arrived safely at Alicante airport.

Matt stretched as he stood up. 'The minute we get

off this damn plane I need a decent cup of coffee and a pee.'

'You could get both of those on the flight.'

'Rubbish. I'm not paying four quid for airplane coffee. And these loos are a) revolting and b) completely hopeless when you're six foot three.'

Sara chuckled. The flight had been smooth, and their luggage was travelling on to Barcelona, so they didn't have to lug it around with them. Matt reached easily into the overhead locker and handed Sara her shoulder bag and the extremely well wrapped painting. They joined the penguin shuffle for the stairs to the ground.

Once in the airport, Matt spotted the sign for the gents. 'You'll be all right for two minutes?'

Sara nodded. 'I'll wait over there by the escalator.'

Matt nipped off, and Sara wandered slowly towards the top of the escalator, reading all the sudden texts that dropped into her mobile informing her about roaming costs. As she stopped at the top of the staircase, a man suddenly barged into her, and snatched her bag, wrenching it from her shoulder and breaking the strap. Sara screamed, and heads turned. The painting, knocked from her grasp, flew through the air and started tumbling down the escalator, bouncing as it went.

Two more men shot past her; Matt, and a guy in a black suit. They leapt on to the escalator, desperately pushing and shoving people aside, racing to catch the package before it became a mangled heap in the mechanism where the stairs got swallowed at the bottom of the flight. Sara watching, horrified, saw Matt snatch up the parcel, almost overbalancing on the steep flight as he did so. The other man made a grab for the painting, but Matt hung on grimly. A swift punch sent him reeling, and the suited man snatched the picture, leapt off the escalator and started to run up the 'up' flight. He presented his trophy to Sara with a slight bow.

'Your parcel, Senora.'

Matt, bleeding and panting hard was there just seconds later.

'What the fuck—?'

'You know this man?'

'Yes I know him —' Sara was furious, indignant. 'Who the hell are you? Why did you hit him? Are you all right, Matt?'

Matt was pressing a wedge of tissues to his nose and lip. He nodded, pulling the tissues away, looking at the blood and then pressing them back again.

'Senor, my apologies. I believed you were the thief. Please, let me help you.' He spoke rapidly into his phone, and Sara and Matt were escorted to some seats by a couple more of the black-suited men. Yet another politely handed Sara her shoulder bag.

'I'm afraid the strap has been broken, Senora. We have the man. He has taken nothing out. We will of course, compensate you for the damage.' He looked at Matt. 'Again, my sincere apologies, Senor. We will get you some ice, immediately.' He clicked his fingers and one of the dark-suited men scurried off. 'Please, both of you, come this way. Senor Garcia has a car waiting for you.'

'You're Garcia's men?'

'Si. I fear he will be upset that we have hurt your friend. Again, please accept my most sincere apologies.'

Sara felt Matt take a firm grip of her hand, and they walked silently through the airport, flanked by the men in black. Nobody looked at the group. In fact, Sara thought, everyone made conscious efforts to look elsewhere. There was a definite air of menace about Garcia's men.

At the airport door, three sleek black Mercedes drew up. The first and last remained where they were, their doors shut, but the driver leapt silently out of the middle car and bowed slightly, opening the rear door and indicating that they should get in. As Matt bent to get into the car, one of the men approached him with an apologetic air. 'Your ice, Senor.' Matt accepted the pack without a word. They sat in the back, still holding hands, intimidated, but determined not to show it. Other cars moved out of the way as their cavalcade went past. It wasn't long before the car stopped and the driver opened the door for Sara.

'This way, please, Mrs Parker, Senor.'

Sara looked at Matt and beckoned him to follow her through the glass doors and into a silent, carpeted lift. Pressing a button, the driver stared straight ahead as the elevator whizzed smoothly up. Sara watched the floor numbers: 14, 15, 16, 17, 18.

'Through the double doors at the end, please. Senor Garcia is expecting you.'

Gritting her teeth and pulling herself to her full five-foot-five, Sara walked down the corridor like a warrior queen about to face the barbarian hordes. As she reached them, the doors opened silently, spooking her a little, but her pace barely hesitated.

Sitting behind a shining mahogany desk, an ordinary-looking man in his middle thirties got to his feet politely.

'Mrs Parker? And Mr Lincoln? Welcome to my humble abode.' He laughed. 'Isn't that what the bad guys in films always say? Please, first let me apologise for the appalling welcome you received at the airport. The thief has been dealt with, and obviously, you will allow me to settle all your bills while you are in my country, by way of compensation for your treatment at the hands of my staff.'

Matt raised his eyebrows. Sara wondered what 'dealt with' meant. She strongly suspected that it might have hurt. Clearly Garcia wasn't expecting them to refuse his offer.

Three walls of the vast room were glass, affording a stunning view over the city and miles beyond, with a glimmer of the sea in the far distance.

'Welcome, anyway. Can I offer you a drink? A brandy, to settle the nerves? A glass of cava, perhaps? No? A coffee, then?'

He nodded to one of the men standing at the door. 'Three coffees, por favor.'

Matt steadied the parcel on the table but kept hold of it with one hand. He sniffed and dabbed at his nose again.

'This is the Sorolla? I can't wait to see it. It can join some of its friends.'

245

Garcia indicated the wall behind them, arrayed like a gallery. Sara was sure one of the paintings was a Goya, and she recognised a Miro in the top corner. A space had been left, at eye height, slightly right of centre on the wall.

'You can see I'm already eager to hang it.'

He introduced the tall man who joined them as the lackey entered, carrying a steaming pot of coffee and three exquisite bone china cups on a tray.

'This is my legal advisor. He is able to check through all your documentation.' He didn't tell them the man's name.

'As Mr Lincoln will check through yours.'

'Of course.'

Garcia escorted Sara to the window, where he started pointing out landmarks as though he hadn't a care in the world, and she was merely a visitor he was entertaining with delight and pride in his city. Weirdly, a phrase from Sunday school wandered through Sara's mind. "All the kingdoms of the world I can show to you…"

Behind them, Matt and the lawyer scrutinised each other's papers.

'So, you will go on to visit Barcelona next, I hear.'

Sara had no idea HOW he knew this, but decided not to rise to the bait. She smiled pleasantly.

'That's right. I'm going to queue for hours in the heat to see the Sagrada Familia again. See how it's getting along.'

'Oh yes. A magnificent creation. Gaudi had such genius. I envy you your visit.' He had no discernable

246

accent at all. Behind them the lawyer nodded. Garcia caught the movement reflected in the window.

'You are both content?'

'Yes.'

'Si.'

'Good. May I?'

Sara looked at Matt, who nodded again. She passed the painting over.

Garcia unwrapped the parcel with great care, and studied the picture for a full two minutes before he looked up. The miles of bubble-wrap that Sara had insisted on had done their job, and the painting was undamaged from its impromptu journey down the escalator. Although she had nothing to hide, Sara could feel her heart beating faster.

Garcia looked at Sara calmly. 'And you paid how much for this?'

'My husband took it for a debt.'

'I am aware of that. But yet you bought it at the house sale. How much?'

Sara licked her lips. 'I knocked them down to thirty euros.'

'Thirty euros. I see.' He took his wallet from an inside pocket. For one terrible moment, Sara had thought that he was reaching for a gun. With delicacy, he placed three ten-euro notes on the desk.

'I don't see why you should be out of pocket for your husband's foolishness, Mrs Parker.'

There was the merest hint of humour flickering in the man's eye. 'Please, let me compensate you.'

Sara raised her eyebrows at him and he laughed.

Straight faced, she picked up the money, folded it, and put it in the back pocket of her jeans.

'Ah, no, Mrs Parker. Another thief, a pickpocket, will take it. There are some real criminals out there.' Laughing, he handed her the documents. 'These release your husband from his debts. I will settle the hospital bill, also. Advise him, please, that he will not be welcome in my casinos in future, though. In fact, it might be wise for him not to return to Spain at all. Or perhaps it won't be you that gives him that advice?'

'I'll tell Micaela.'

'How remarkably civilised. Tell Ms Fernandez also, then, that a private plane will transport both her and her "husband",' here he drew inverted commas in the air, 'out of my country and into London City airport the day after tomorrow. I am not without connections. Thank you for your time.'

He shook her hand.

'Mr Lincoln. Again, please accept my utmost apologies.' He inclined his head in an old-fashioned way. Matt held the bloody tissues out to one of the silent henchmen. He took them without a flicker of emotion, and continued to hold his silent pose by the door.

As they descended in the rapid lift, Matt squeezed Sara's hand. They politely refused the offer of a lift back to the airport, and walked up the street without speaking. At the corner Sara turned to Matt.

'Nerves of steel,' she said shakily, holding out her hands, which trembled slightly. He took them in his own warm grasp.

'He was bloody terrifying. All that menace. And he can't have been much older than thirty-five. What does he eat for breakfast, orphans? Do you need a drink as much as I do?'

'I rather think I do.' Sara thought about the luggage that they'd left at the airport, ready for this afternoon's connection to Barcelona. 'Shall we go back to the bar at the Aeroport d'Alacant? Senor Garcia would no doubt buy us a couple of large glasses of celebratory bubbles, at the very least.' Tentatively, wincing, she raised her fingers to his face, her touch barely feathering over his split lip. 'Does it hurt much?'

'Does it give me a heroic aspect?' He gave her a sideways glance.

'Absolutely. I think the very least I can do is buy you a stiff drink.'

'No "ministering angel" bit then?'

'Later.' Her voice was warm.

Matt nodding, held up his arm. 'Taxi.'

Be Careful What You Wish For

Micaela fluttered round Graham as they sat in the little plane. It was smarter than anything she'd ever flown in before, and far, far newer. Graham accepted her tlc without a word. He was still very pale, and he tired easily. Losing a toe made him wobble slightly when he made certain movements, and he was clearly still in shock about that. They'd told him that he'd soon compensate his movement. Micaela wasn't sure he'd quite understood. She'd arranged for a taxi to pick them up and take them back to her flat at the other end. They'd have to sort out better living accommodation one way or the other, though. Micaela was unwilling to put down roots in England, she needed the sun. Already, she'd mentioned the possibility of applying for a job in Adelaide. He hadn't leapt at the idea, but he hadn't actually said no, either. Some strange dream he had had while he was ill was clearly pressing on his mind, and he'd had the same dream a couple of times since, as well.

'I do trust you, Micaela,' he'd said. 'I know you'll look after me.'

She wasn't sure that she was over-fond of this new dependant Graham, but reasoned that he'd had a brush with death, which had indirectly been her fault, so she'd put up with it for now. She doubted it would last long. The old ebullient Graham would doubtless resurface with one brilliant moneymaking scheme or another, as soon as he possibly could.

She was rather more concerned about *that* Graham.

Six weeks had passed since the night of the frightening phone call and life had settled into its new pattern. Janet was now occupying the big bedroom at the front of Martha's house—the room that had once been Graham's. After much deliberation, she and Martha had decided to try it for a few months and see how it went, rather than rushing in to anything permanent. So far, it was working for both of them.

Sara's house was on the market. If she had plans, she was keeping them to herself, but it was generally supposed that they involved Matt Lincoln. He was saying nothing either. It was very frustrating for the gossip-mongers in the office.

In Gloucester Quays, two women were sitting in the Caffe Nero, watching the door, alert to every entrance and exit. Micaela had arranged to be in there with Graham between eleven and twelve.

'We don't have to speak to him,' Jude had said. 'He doesn't even know that we'll be in there. We can just see how we feel. It might just help if we can see he's OK. We'll know what we want to do after we see him, I'm sure.'

Martha nodded. When it had been suggested to her, she'd thought it was a good idea. Now, she wasn't sure that she could do this. Janet had warned her against it, and Dilys had been vociferous about what she saw as "Yet another damn-fool errand". Perhaps they were right. This was a mistake. As she was about to get to her feet and leave, the ever-elegant Micaela walked in, slightly in front of a skinny, greying man with a receding hairline and a petulant expression. He favoured one foot as he threaded his way across the café, clutching at the furniture and lifting his foot protectively when anyone moved closer to him.

'But Mic, I don't WANT a bloody coffee,' he was complaining. 'Why can't we just go and watch the rugby like you promised? I don't know why you want to come to a crumbling dump like Gloucester anyway.'

'Sit down, Graham. I want a coffee, even if you don't. If I have to stand in a rugby ground being deafened all afternoon, I need plenty of caffeine first. Do you want a Danish?' She indicated the counter, where cakes and pastries were arranged in tempting rows.

'I need a beer.' He slumped grumpily into the leather bucket chair and rested his foot on the table. Blithely, Micaela lifted his foot higher and shoved a magazine under it. He ignored her. 'Fine. I'm going to get a flat white and a cinnamon roll.' Micaela spoke to the air above his head, and her tone suggested that this was a long-rumbling argument. 'Nothing for you then?'

Jude looked at Martha and raised her eyebrows.

'What do you think, Martha? Shall we go across and re-introduce ourselves? See what he has to say for himself? See if he would like to apologise and make amends?'

Martha shook her head.

'I wish I hadn't come. Just look at him. That's not my Graham.' She paused, staring at the surly wreck of a man her son had become. 'And yet in another way, I'm glad we did. Without all this, I'd never have found you, or the children.' She squeezed Jude's arm. 'I've got all the family I need, now that I've found you. Graham made his choice years ago, and I think I've just made mine. I'm ready to leave whenever you are, Jude. Is that all right with you?'

'Oh yes. That's fine.' She folded the cover back on the magazine she'd been flicking through and got to her feet, hooking her arm through Martha's as they made their way towards the exit. 'Fancy a bit of shopping while we're here?'

Graham nudged Micaela, pushing his face right up to hers.

'Look at those two over there. D'you reckon she's that old woman's carer? Sexy girl like that, wasting her life looking after an old bag. I reckon this country's had it. Maybe we should go to Oz, Mic. We could get married over there. I bet I could make money out there. What d'you reckon?'

Micaela winced at Graham's sour breath. Once, she would have seized an offer like that with both hands. Now she wasn't so certain. Not certain at all. She looked at the coffee in front of her, and remembered the old proverb: "Be careful what you wish for". Biting into the cinnamon roll, she saw Jude and Martha walking out through the door, and for one swift moment thought about running to join them.

Not for the first time since they came back to England, Micaela wondered if Senor Garcia might welcome an administrator.

Acknowledgements

I'd like to send my thanks to the team at Black Pear Press, especially the ever-patient Polly Stretton, and to everyone who helped, encouraged and cheered from the sidelines—you know who you are. And special thanks to my late and lovely friend Gwyneth Ephraim, who had faith and kept me laughing.

About the Author

Roz Levens describes herself as 'Writer, storyteller and encourager of writing in others.' She runs popular 'Write with Roz' workshops at The Hive in Worcester and in Evesham. She says she has a 25m swimming certificate and gave up dog agility because she couldn't keep up with Reg the dog!

"Roz Levens' work is vicious, in the best way! She has a marvellous tendency to combine crime and comedy, with brilliant results, and she blends this with wonderfully distinct characters too (many of whom often get what they deserve in one way or another). There is something unique about the way Levens puts a story together, and she always manages to introduce the unexpected in her plots—and at exactly the right time.

"A breath of fresh air, regardless of the genre she's leaning towards, Levens' work makes for entertaining reading time and again. *Pack of Lies* is sure to amuse and entertain new and familiar readers alike, and here's hoping this is the first of many novels from this author."

Dr Charley Barnes
Writer in Residence at The Swan Theatre
Worcestershire Poet Laureate 2019-2020
Managing Director | Sabotage Reviews

Publications

Five Short Stories, 'The VSS365 Anthology Vol.1' (bonus chapter contributor by invitation only), Mark A. King (2019)

Short listed: *Malice Aforethought,* also *This Train Terminates Here,* and, *Bad Adelaide,* 'The Jar Thief', Worcs LitFest Flash Fiction, Black Pear Press (2019)

Short listed: *Mediterranean Blue,* also *Des Res,* and, *Shut the Door,* 'Sacrifice', Worcs LitFest Flash Fiction, Black Pear Press (2018)

Comedy section short list: *The First Law of Holes,* 'Flash Fiction Festival', AdHoc Fiction (2018)

Nothing Like a Sunday Roast, 'Wired', Worcs LitFest Flash Fiction, Black Pear Press (2017)

Winner: 'Worcestershire LitFest & Fringe Flash Fiction Slam 2017'

Short listed: *Always Careful, Never Greedy,* 'Evesham Festival of Words (2): Best stories from 2017', Black Pear Press (2017)

Cora's Angel, 'People's Friend', D.C. Thompson (2017)

Whirring Cogs, Finalist: 'The Exeter Story Prize Collection', CreativeWriting Matters (2016)

As Caroline Price:
Flora, 'The Dawntreader', Indigo Dreams (Summer 2019)
Learning Amongst the Leaves, 'Countryside Magazine', Fellows Media (2001)
Co-authored: *Health and Social Care Compulsory Units, Compulsory Units plus Options,* and, *Tutors' File*, Heinemann (2000)